I

The Hollow Alpha

Shifters of Miridia   Book One

Himera Ink

Copyright © 2025 by Himera Ink
Published by Himera Ink
Contact: inkashesink@gmail.com

All rights reserved. No part of this publication may be reproduced, distributed, or transmitted in any form or by any means, including but not limited to photocopying, recording, or other electronic or mechanical methods, without the prior written permission of the author and publisher, except in the case of brief quotations used in reviews and certain other noncommercial uses permitted by copyright law.

This book is a work of fiction. Names, characters, places, and incidents are products of the author's imagination or are used fictitiously. Any resemblance to actual persons, living or dead, or actual events is purely coincidental.

This work may not be used, in whole or in part, for the training, development, or fine-tuning of artificial intelligence systems (AI), language models, or machine learning algorithms without the express written permission of the author and copyright holder.

Book cover credit:
Graphic design and concept: Himera Ink

For permissions or inquiries, please contact:
inkashesink@gmail.com

Disclaimer

This is a work of fiction. All names, characters, organizations, and events portrayed in this book are products of the author's imagination or used fictitiously. Any resemblance to actual persons, living or dead, or real events is purely coincidental.

This book contains fictional depictions of violence and sexual scenes. These depictions are not meant to be instructional or to be used as real-life advice, guidance, or reference.

The author does not condone or promote any harmful behavior described in this book. Any methods portrayed — particularly involving harm, coercion, or illegal acts — should under no circumstances be imitated, replicated, or attempted.

Reader discretion is advised.

A Note From The Author

This book came to life as a way to escape the darkness in my other work — specifically my dark romance series, *Iron Vultures MC*. Sometimes, I need something lighter and a little bit funny to bring the tension down — especially after writing tens of thousands of words filled with pain, despair, and torture.

This story is what you might call a "palate cleanser." It's something to enjoy after a hard day of work, when all you want to do is shut off your brain and relax for a while.

It's short. It's funny. It's also *heartbreak-y* in parts.

I hope you enjoy it!

Also… I CAN'T BELIEVE THIS IS MY SECOND PUBLISHED BOOK! How the hell did this happen?!

That being said, I'm always happy to receive messages and talk to readers. You can contact me at inkashesink@gmail.com

CONTENTS

Prologue	3
Chapter 1	7
Chapter 2	13
Chapter 3	22
Chapter 4	36
Chapter 5	47
Chapter 6	58
Chapter 7	72
Chapter 8	80
Chapter 9	88
Chapter 10	101
Chapter 11	113
Chapter 12	122
Chapter 13	135
Chapter 14	145
Chapter 15	165
Chapter 16	178
Chapter 17	188
Chapter 18	205

Chapter 19	213
Epilogue 1	222
Epilogue 2	225
The End	235
Bonus	236

Blurb

He broke her. And then she broke the rules.

When commoner wolf shifter Kassira is rejected in front of an entire royal ballroom by her fated mate, King Draven, the ruthless Alpha with dragon blood, her world shatters. Banished to the cursed edge of Kunou Forest, she's left to bleed in silence while he continues ruling with another woman on his arm.

But a bond this powerful doesn't die quietly.

Six months later, Kassira is done grieving. She's ready to sever the bond for good. Even if it means breaking herself to do it. But when she finally lets go, Draven's monstrous lycan form awakens... and he doesn't take rejection well.

Especially when the mate he cast aside is no longer his.

PROLOGUE

He looks at me with bored amusement, like I just told a bad joke. There's a smile on his face — polite, perfect. But his eyes… his eyes are sharp. A warning. Cold steel in golden light.

"What did you just say?" His voice is slow, measured. Mocking. Like I'm a child who said something foolish and he's humoring me before I'm dismissed.

"You're my mate." I whisper it. A prayer. A mistake.

The moment the words leave my mouth, I know I shouldn't have said them. Not here. Not now. The ballroom is too bright, too crowded, and filled with the kind of people who feast on weakness. But I couldn't stop myself. The moment he walked in, my soul screamed. The bond ignited so fast it scorched me. Couldn't he feel it, too?

He laughs — quiet, empty. The sound slices through the growing hush of the crowd. Heads turn. Conversations die. I feel a bead of sweat trail down my spine, my wolf coiled inside me, on high alert. "*Something is wrong,*" she whispers.

He leans in slightly, his voice dipping, but not enough. Not enough to hide us from the ears now trained on every word.

"I don't have a mate," he says. The amusement is gone. What's left is frost. "Everyone knows this. Maybe this is your idea of a joke, or maybe you're just trying to climb your way into power. A power you clearly don't understand."

I open my mouth, but nothing comes out. My lips tremble. I can feel my pulse in my throat, in my ears, in my chest.

His eyes harden.

"Even if, by some miracle, I had a mate... it wouldn't be a pathetic, weak little thing like you."

Gasps ripple through the crowd. I flinch. My chest tightens, like a noose just slipped around my ribs.

He says it loud enough for everyone to hear. On purpose.

My eyes blur, but I don't let the tears fall. Not yet.

"What even are you?" he sneers, looking me up and down like filth clinging to his boots. "There's not even an ounce of power in you, and you dare approach me?"

A single heartbeat of silence. And then a quiet, cruel chuckle comes from somewhere in the crowd. Snickers follow. Whispers. Eyes on me like knives.

My heart shatters, the bond twisting in my chest like barbed wire. My wolf whimpers inside me, clawing at the walls of my soul. *"He's ours,"* she says. *"Why doesn't he feel it? Why won't he see?"*

He takes a step forward.

"You leave now," he says, voice low and dangerous, "or I'll have my men drag you out."

I can't breathe. I can't speak. My body starts to shake. I take a step back, but he catches it — the fear. His finger twitches. For one terrifying moment, I think he might strike me. The king. My mate. The man fate gave me.

Then her hand slides into his — small, pale, perfect. The woman beside him. Regal. Red-haired. Radiating so much power my spine almost bows.

"Draven, darling," she says sweetly, her voice a melody. "Ignore her. We have more important things to do."

He's still staring at me.

And in his eyes now? Something darker. Like he does feel it, and he hates it.

She tugs at him gently. He looks down at her and softens, smiling like she's the only one that matters.

"I'll be right with you, love."

And then he kisses her softly.

That's when it happens.

A searing pain rips through my chest, folding me in half. I clutch at my heart, my knees buckling. The bond is burning, fracturing, howling. My soul screams in agony.

A tear slips down my cheek. I meet his gaze one last time.

He looks at me like I'm nothing. Like I'm a bug that

should be squashed.

"You're still here." His voice is flat, final. "Guards. Take her away. I'll deal with her later."

They come. Strong hands grip my arms.

And I let them. Because I'm too stunned, too embarrassed, too much in pain to fight them. No one has ever rejected their mate. It's the law.

CHAPTER 1

Kassira

Six Months Later

I watch him pass by. Imposing. Powerful. Proud. The sun catches on his dark hair, the sharp lines of his jaw, the broad strength of his shoulders wrapped in black and gold. His steps are measured, confident. The kind of walk only a king has. The kind of presence only he has.

Something tightens in my chest. Familiar and *hated.*

He doesn't look at me. Doesn't even glance in my direction. But he knows I'm here. Of course he does. It would be impossible for him to not feel me so close.

Because I'm his bonded. His mate. The one he rejected and cast into the dirt, disgust etched into his face. I'm right here, lost to the darkness where he exiled me. At the edge of this cursed land of the forsaken. The unworthy. The outcasts. The ones not good enough to breathe the same air as the crown. The one and only Kunou Forest, where sunlight doesn't dare reach the ground.

That's what he thinks of me. Too dirty to touch someone like him. Too weak to deserve his name on my skin. Too nothing.

But *she* isn't.

She walks beside him like she was born for it. Beautiful. Regal. The red of her hair catching fire in the wind. Her smile is easy. Practiced. Like poisoned honey.

She doesn't feel the ache that haunts my every step. She doesn't lie awake at night hearing a bond that won't stop screaming. She doesn't have to claw her way back to life every morning.

I do.

I've spent six months in pain since the night he shattered me in front of the entire court. Six months living in exile, gathering every scrap of magic buried in my blood.

My power may be faint, fractured... but it's mine. And it's enough.

Enough to do what must be done. Enough to maybe keep me alive after this.

I raise my hand slowly. My fingers tremble — not from fear, but from the weight of what's coming. Neris shifts inside me, her energy pulsing with mine, wild and ready.

We speak as one. It's what always has to happen to truly destroy a bond. The wolf and the human must both agree.

"I sever this bond."

The words fall from our mouths like a blade through silk. My magic rises, pale and trembling, wrapping around the bond tethering me to him. The invisible thread connecting our souls pulls taut, then—

It snaps.

I feel it ripping my chest apart, stealing my breath away.

Somewhere in the distance, Draven stumbles. His head jerks. His hand flies to his chest like he's been pierced with a blade no one else can see.

I watch him. And then watch her reach for him, confused.

"Draven?" her voice rises in panic. "Draven, what's wrong?"

He doesn't answer.

He roars. Wild. Feral.

The sound tears through the air, raw and primal and deafening. The very ground trembles beneath my feet. Trees groan. The wind dies.

The sky splits in half. Windows shatter. Birds scatter away, knowing what's to come. A woman screams somewhere behind the market stalls.

And then he shifts.

Bones break. Muscle tears. Magic rips through the air in waves that shake the cobblestones.

One second of silence follows, so heavy it feels like the town itself is bracing for death.

And then a lycan comes forward. Not a wolf!

Holy shit! My eyes are about to pop out of my skull.

He erupts out of Draven like wildfire out of stone. Ten feet tall. At least. Muscles rippling in fury under black fur. Claws that glint like obsidian. His wings unfurl behind him like a storm made of flesh. Each flap sends debris flying. Market tents collapse. Horses rear and bolt. People run, scream, dive behind anything that might keep them alive.

He unleashes a howl that doesn't sound like pain.

It sounds like rage. Like loss. Like pure madness. It's a sound that doesn't belong in this world. It shouldn't exist.

People don't stop screaming.

He slams a clawed fist into the cobblestone, and the ground splinters. Shards of stone crack upward like jagged teeth. He reaches for a wagon and throws it into a building without hesitation. Wood explodes. Flames catch. Smoke starts to billow.

I feel every ounce of his rage like a phantom pressing into my chest. It wasn't just pain. The bond didn't just snap. It shattered him.

Guards rush in, but it's a mistake. They don't last.

He swipes one aside with a single claw and sends the man flying across the square. The next is crushed instantly. Another tries to shift mid-air, but the lycan grabs him by the throat and throws him through a bakery window.

Shit. That used to be my bakery.

I flinch, but I don't look away. I can't look away. Neris is entranced, too.

Because we feel him. Not just his rage. His grief.

The animal inside him is unraveling. Tearing through control and logic like it's paper. And the worst part?

He still doesn't know why.

Amira screams Draven's name, her hands glowing, magic forming in her palms. She tries to cast something — I don't know what — but the second the lycan sees her, he snarls. Wings spread wide. He doesn't attack, but she freezes.

She starts backing away with wide, terrified eyes. There's nothing she can do. She is not the lycan's mate. She cannot tame him. Some part of her knows she's lost him. The king.

The lycan suddenly goes still in the center of the chaos. Amid fire and dust and blood.

His head lifts slowly. Nostrils flare. And then his eyes — burning molten silver, laced with black — turn.

Toward me. "Shit," I whisper under my breath.

The forest's shadow brushes the town's edge. I stand just beyond it, my hand still lifted, heart still aching.

And in that one breathless moment, he sees me.

Really sees me.

The bond may be gone. But the echo of it? The memory of what we were meant to be?

It's still there and I see the exact second it slams into

him, powerful and undeniable.

A sound leaves his throat — half snarl, half sob. His wings falter. He stumbles, just once.

And then he starts to move toward me.

I turn fast, ready to run. But the moment I take the first step, I sway. The severing of the bond took too much out of me. I knew this might happen, but I had to take the risk.

"Neris, we need to run," I say to my wolf but it's too late. She's already fading in and out of consciousness. Just like me.

I start falling but before I reach the ground, strong arms grab me.

"No," is the last word I whisper before I'm lost to the darkness.

CHAPTER 2

Kassira

I wake up with a headache that feels like my brain's boiling inside my skull.

And then — just as suddenly — it's gone. Silence. Stillness. Huh. That's good.

My eyes are closed, but my hand is already searching. The texture beneath me isn't familiar — too soft, too smooth, too damn expensive. This isn't the rough cot in my home in Kunou Forest. This isn't exile.

Then it hits me all at once. The memories. What I've done. What I've unleashed.

My eyes snap open. I sit up too fast and nearly choke on a gasp.

The bed I'm in? It looks like it belongs to a royal. No, not even that. It looks like it belongs to a god. Rich, dark wood. Velvet sheets. Pillows made of clouds, probably stitched by angels or fae seamstresses or something. It's disgustingly perfect.

I don't get to enjoy it long.

A low snarl rumbles through the room.

My head jerks toward the sound, and my blood turns to ice.

A massive, winged lycan crouches in the corner, silver eyes glowing, teeth bared. His jaws are too big to fully close, drool pooling beneath him in thick, wet strings. His wings twitch like he's trying not to pounce.

Oh, stars. This is fine. Everything's fine. Except for the GIANT MONSTER watching me like I'm a walking steak.

I reach inside for Neris. Nothing. She's still unconscious. I'm alone.

And alone, I'm useless.

Not that she could fight a lycan. Not even a tiny one. But still — her presence always made me feel braver. Now it's just me. My fear. My heartbeat pounding in my ears.

I take a slow breath and move to slide out of the bed, my eyes locked on the beast.

The moment my foot touches the floor, he snarls — louder this time, guttural and sharp.

I scramble backward into the pillows, heart galloping.

"Do not snarl at me," I hiss, my voice barely a whisper but laced with shaky defiance. "That's rude."

He huffs, big gusts of air shooting from his nostrils like warning flares. His ears flick. His tail lashes. He's not amused.

Fantastic. I escaped a cursed bond only to become the

personal chew toy of a deranged lycan.

I scan the room, taking it in properly now. Ornate. Opulent. Every inch screams royalty, from the gilded fireplace to the crystal decanter on the nightstand.

My stomach drops. Why didn't I think of this when I was admiring the bed?

I narrow my eyes at the monster in front of me. "Is this your room?"

He blinks once. Slowly. Then — he rolls his eyes.

He rolls. His eyes. At me.

"I knew it!" I say, the horror crawling up my throat. "You brought me to your room! You — You had sex with her in this bed, didn't you?!"

My voice cracks. I start breathing faster.

"I need to get out of here. I need to leave."

I make the mistake of moving again.

He lunges — not to attack, but to stop me. One massive clawed hand lands on my shoulder. I freeze. His talons graze skin. A single flex, and I'm ribbons. Tiny ribbons.

He leans in. Close. Too close. His snout hovers in front of my nose. I can feel the heat of his breath. The weight of his gaze.

And then... he sniffs.

He gestures with his head. A small flick toward the room.

I frown. "You want me to... smell something?"

He growls.

"I swear, if you're making me sniff your dirty secrets —"

But his claws are still on me, and my survival instinct says *cooperate*.

So I inhale.

And it's clean. Just clean. And…also familiar. It smells like Draven. Like smoke and fire and the edge of something dark.

Nothing else.

I deflate slightly, my pulse slowing. The lycan pulls back. Just a little.

"Maaattte."

I go completely still.

He speaks? HE SPEAKS?! No lycan or wolf can speak!

The sound is rough, broken. A growl laced with something deeper. Something that rumbles in my bones. My eyes widen. "You… what?"

He stares at me, unwavering.

"I am not your mate," I snap, arms crossed over my chest.

He rolls his eyes. Again.

I gasp. "Stop doing that! It's rude!"

He huffs again and brings his snout even closer.

"Maaaattteee," he repeats, softer this time. Almost

like… a plea.

Something shivers down my spine.

Okay. No. No, no. I've definitely snapped something loose in my brain.

I push at his snout. It takes both hands — his nose is bigger than my face.

He lets me.

Courage rises like a tide inside me. "You won't hurt me," I whisper. "If you wanted to, you would've done it already."

He doesn't move. Just watches.

I narrow my eyes. "How well can you speak? Can you do sentences?"

He tilts his head. Shakes it slightly.

"Of course not," I mutter. "Because that would be too convenient."

I look closer into his eyes, and that's when it clicks.

"He's not home, is he?" I whisper. "Draven. He's not… in there. You're not connected right now."

The lycan nods once, slowly.

"Shit."

A lycan unanchored from its human side? That's the stuff of nightmares. Dangerous. Unpredictable. One wrong move and I'm a stain on these very expensive sheets.

I'm about to really panic when I feel her, flickering like

a soft spark in the back of my mind. Neris.

"Ask him his name," she yawns, like we're not currently locked in a room with a feral apex predator.

"Neris." My voice softens. "You okay?"

"Never been better. No bond to pull at me until everything hurts, no pain with every heartbeat." She sounds lighter. Brighter. *"We're free, Kass. We're finally free."*

Something in my chest warms. I smile. It's brief, but real.

My gaze shifts back to the monster in front of me. My hand is still on his snout. He hasn't moved. Just stares at me like he's waiting for me to do something. Say something.

"What's your name?" I ask.

He rumbles low in his throat, then speaks, voice thick and broken: "Drrraaaxissss."

A hiss and a snarl wrapped into one. Rough, but clear enough.

"Okay. Draxis." I nod. "Now we're getting somewhere."

He watches me expectantly. Eager. Still too close.

"I need to get out of here."

He doesn't move. Just shakes his head once. "Maaattteee."

That damn word again.

"No, Draxis. No." I cross my arms. "I am not your mate. You're just glitching right now. You need to get on the same page with your other half."

He growls low — not angry. Just... stubborn.

"Bring Draven forward," I command, lifting my chin. "I want to speak to him. Now."

Another shake of his massive head. Again with the defiance.

"I swear to the gods, I'll scream."

He puffs a breath into my face — hot and unimpressed. My threat means nothing to him.

Because he knows no one would come for me. Who would take on a huge beast for little ol' me?

"Let me at him," Neris growls inside me. *"He can't keep us here like this. We broke the bond. He has no right."*

Before I can say anything else, Draxis whines.

A high, soft sound. Pitiful. Like a puppy.

He leans closer, slowly stretching his massive neck toward me. His eyes are pleading. Another whine. Then — he lifts a talon and scratches at his neck.

He wants something.

"What — what is it? Do you want me to scratch you?" I blink. "Seriously?"

But then I see it. A flicker. A shimmer beneath the fur.

My breath catches. My hand moves on instinct.

I brush aside the thick, black hair at the side of his neck, and my stomach drops.

A collar.

Deep red. Almost molten. Etched with strange markings. So tightly latched I never saw it through the fur. It pulses faintly with magic. Faint... but old. Dangerous.

I reach out, just one finger. The moment I touch it — zap!

Pain bites through me like lightning. I yank my hand back.

"What is this thing?" I whisper, staring at him.

Draxis whines again, scraping at his neck with growing desperation.

"I don't know how to help you." My voice wavers. "You need to bring Draven forward. Maybe he knows what this is. Maybe you two can fix it. Together."

He stares at me like I've gutted him. Like I've betrayed him. Big, googly, full-on puppy eyes. And stars, it goes straight to my heart — this is why I never got a dog.

"I'm not your magic solution, Draxis. I can't break this, I don't have that kind of power."

He growls, frustrated this time. Angry. But not at me.

I straighten, steel sliding into my spine.

"You need Draven," I say firmly. "Let him in. Now."

His silver eyes narrow, defiant.

We lock stares. Neither of us blinking. Neither of us willing to budge.

But I don't back down. I keep staring.

Finally, he huffs. His body shudders. And then his eyes flicker. Molten silver fades to cold steel blue. And the shift begins.

Bones snap. Fur recedes. Wings collapse inward. He drops to his knees, trembling.

In a matter of seconds, he's here.

Draven.

Completely human. Completely naked. On the floor at my feet.

CHAPTER 3

Draven

My head is spinning.

The shift. The rage. The lycan.

It shouldn't have happened. What the hell was that?

I remember it in bits and pieces, before the beast shoved me away and locked me inside my own mind.

I've never turned into a lycan before. I thought I couldn't shift fully. I thought I was something else — something in-between. A king with wings. Magic. Power. Strength.

But not that.

I was ten when the wings came. The scales. The flame under my skin. Everyone said it was my dragon blood awakening, what I inherited from my father.

And when I didn't shift fully at sixteen like other shifters, they said I just didn't have a wolf, the part of me that I could have inherited from my mother. And I didn't have a dragon, either. Just the wings, the strength and the magic. The lycan part was never even considered. Too distant in lineage to rise.

I was more than powerful enough to win all challenges and take my throne, though. The first Alpha King without a shifted form.

But if I have a lycan, why did it come forward just now? Eighteen years later than it should have? I should have shifted completely at ten. That's when lycans come forward. Earlier than any other shifter. They're the most impatient ones and the quickest to anger.

A deep pain settles inside me, wrapping around my heart like a vine made of thorns. It feels like someone took a blade made of fire and drove it straight through my chest — then twisted. Over and over. The bond isn't gone. It's still there, shredded and bleeding. Torn from the inside out. Every breath feels like inhaling acid. My magic is scattered, panicked, like it doesn't know where to go. My soul claws at my insides, trying to reach for her end of the bond. But it finds nothing. The emptiness is maddening. Louder than pain. A silence so complete it roars.

I look down.

A bruise blooms at the center of my chest, dark and angry.

She really is my mate.

It's the only word the lycan was screaming inside my skull before everything went black. Over and over. *Mate. Mate. Mate.* Until it was all I could hear.

And I rejected her.

I rejected my own mate.

She severed the bond. Cut it clean. And now there's this gaping hole where something sacred should be.

How is that even possible? How did I not feel it before? How did I not know?

I lift my head and meet her gaze.

She watches me with wary, narrowed eyes.

She's perched high on the bed, regal in her defiance. And me? I'm on my knees on the cold floor beneath her.

Fitting.

Before I can even open my mouth to say anything, she lifts a pillow and chucks it straight at my chest.

"Cover yourself, Your Majesty," she says flatly. "No one wants to see your royal jewels."

I blink.

She's not crying. Not begging. Not even curious. There's none of the pain I'm feeling on her side. She looks at me like I'm just another problem to deal with. Like I'm just something mildly annoying.

I remember her from six months ago.

She was different that night — quiet, hesitant. But even then, there was something about her... something that made me pause. Something that curled around my instincts and told me not to strike. I could've ordered her execution. Could've had her tossed in a dungeon and forgotten. But I didn't. I remember saying the word *exile*, but it felt like it came from somewhere else — like someone was speaking through me, pulling the strings of my mouth while I watched from behind my own eyes.

At the same time, something inside me slammed shut.

Every time I tried to think about her afterward — to question why her presence rattled me, why I kept feeling her everywhere — my thoughts slipped away like smoke. I couldn't hold onto them. Couldn't hold onto her. It was like my mind refused to let her in... and I couldn't ask why.

"I could have killed you. The lycan was feral," I murmur, getting up slowly, pillow strategically placed. My voice is hoarse. Raw.

She rolls her eyes. "Yeah, well. You didn't. So congrats."

"You don't feel it?" I ask. My fingers twitch against the pillow. "The bond. It's still there. You really are my mate."

She shrugs, moving. "Nope. That sounds like a you problem. I solved mine." She stands from the bed and starts pacing the room, scanning for an exit.

"I'm sorry," I say, voice low, rough.

She freezes.

Her eyes snap to mine — sharp and cold enough to draw blood. I swallow hard. Fuck, I need her to understand. I need to make this right.

"I didn't know you were my mate," I say. "I couldn't feel the bond."

I pause, glancing down at the deep bruise across my chest. The skin is dark and aching, but it's nothing compared to what's clawing at my insides.

"I can feel it now," I whisper.

She crosses her arms, one brow raised.

"Too bad. So sad." Her tone is flat. Unbothered. "It doesn't matter anymore."

"Yes, it does!" My head snaps up. "When the High Priestess of the Moon tested me for the Mate Spark — before what should've been my first shift — there was nothing. No trace. I thought I didn't have a mate. I thought I wasn't meant for one. And I couldn't feel my bond to you. Not until now. Someone clearly tampered with it. With me. And what you did—"

I cross my arms across my chest. "What you did is illegal. Severing a bond like that — it's forbidden. It's the law."

She immediately looks to the ceiling, hands fisted, lips pressed tightly like she can barely restrain herself from cursing me out.

"For the love of — can you please put on some pants? Or a sheet? Or something? Stop flashing your ding-a-ling at me!"

She makes an aggressive little flicking motion toward me, as if she's trying to ward off an angry spirit.

My... *ding-a-ling*?

I blink. "Seriously?"

Shifters don't care about nudity. It's not a thing. We're running around naked all the time.

I head toward the closet anyway, speaking over my shoulder as I move. "Did you know about my lycan?"

"Draxis," she says flatly.

I pause. "What?"

"You mean Draxis." Her tone is calm, matter-of-fact. "That's his name, isn't it? And by the way, he needs training. He's very stubborn."

I freeze, one hand halfway through zipping up my pants.

"Training?" I repeat slowly, turning to face her. "A lycan?"

She just shrugs. "Yeah. Training. He needs to learn how to listen."

Is she being serious right now?

"I've never shifted before," I tell her, voice low. "Not once. Even now, I can't feel him in my head. I can't talk to him. It's like… he's gone." I exhale hard, jaw clenched. "The moment you severed the bond—"

Pain punches through my chest so hard I nearly double over. I grind my teeth and breathe through it.

"The moment you did what you did," I say again, steadier this time, "that was the first time he ever came out."

She tilts her head, expression unreadable. Her eyes scan mine like I'm a puzzle she's trying to solve.

"So you didn't just hide him?" she asks. "Because he's different?"

"No," I snap. "Of course not. Why would I—?" I stop. "Did you know about him before? Did your wolf feel him?"

She shakes her head slowly, eyes dimming just a little. Her voice is softer now.

"You need to figure your stuff out," she says. "Your lycan is magically leashed."

My blood runs cold. "What?"

She taps a finger against her own neck. "There's some really old magic wrapped around him. Deep. Powerful. You need to find someone who can help you untangle it. Because that collar? It's probably why you've never shifted. Why you can't hear him. Why everything about you feels off."

Fuck. What the fuck? Leashed? This is bad. So bad.

But so is the fact that I rejected my mate.

"I'm sorry," I say, voice thick. "For the rejection. For all of it. I'll make it right, I swear it. Whatever you need — whatever it takes — I'll do it."

By the end, my voice is frayed. Torn apart.

I can't lose her. Not now. Not when I finally know what she is to me.

She looks at me unimpressed.

"No, thank you," she says simply. "I just want to leave."

That's it. Cold. Clean. Like ice.

"That's not an option," I growl, the sound raw in my throat.

I step toward her. She lifts her hand, palm out, warning me off. I don't stop. I keep moving until her hand presses flat against my chest — right over the bruise.

The second her skin touches mine, the pain inside me eases. Just like that.

My breath catches. I almost fall to my knees.

But she yanks her hand away like I burned her. Her face twists with fury.

"I don't owe you anything," she spits. "I understand now that there's probably some ancient spell screwing with your side of the bond — great. That's your problem, though. It doesn't undo what you did. It doesn't erase what I went through."

She steps back, chin high, voice trembling with rage.

"I went through six months of agony. While you played king and cuddled your girlfriend, I was trying to hold myself together in exile. My wolf and I? We're good now. We're finally free. And you?" Her smile is sharp. "You still have a girlfriend. Go play house with her. I'll find someone else. And we'll both live happily ever after — separately."

The growl that tears out of me is pure instinct. It rattles the room. Cracks through the walls.

Her finger jabs up under my nose so fast it stuns me.

"None of that," she snaps. "Don't you dare pull some alpha possessiveness bullshit on me. Answer the question — did you or did you not have sex with your little girlfriend while I was lost in Kunou Forest, trying to survive?"

The fury in her voice could level a kingdom.

"I didn't," I say, voice low. Steady. True.

She blinks.

"What?" she asks, the fight stalling just slightly behind her eyes.

"I didn't sleep with anyone," I say quietly. "Not once these past six months."

I pause, jaw tightening. I can't tell her the whole truth now, can I? It would bury me further. The words spill out of me though, the sound forced through my mouth before I can even process it.

"I tried, but I couldn't… perform."

What just happened? Why did I admit to that?

I look down — and of course, now there's a very visible issue pressing against my pants.

I throw my hands up, exasperated. "Clearly that's not a problem anymore!"

Her eyebrows shoot so high they practically touch her hairline.

And then she laughs.

It bursts out of her like sunlight breaking through thunderclouds — bright, sharp, and wild. It hits me like a blow to the chest. I'm frozen, caught in it. That sound. I could drown in it and never want air again.

She wipes an imaginary tear from the corner of her eye, smile still curling at the edges of her lips.

"Good," she says, biting each word. "That's great, actually. If your body only reacts to me now, you should go ahead and prepare for a very long, very sexless life."

A low growl rumbles out of me, involuntary.

She doesn't flinch.

Her hand lands on her hip, her expression carved from stone.

"Maybe you didn't screw her," she says, voice like frostbite, "but you still kissed her. Touched her. Held her."

She steps closer, just enough to twist the knife.

"And I felt it. Every. Single. Time." Her voice dips, sharp and gutted. "Every kiss. Every touch. It tore through me. A betrayal to our bond. I can't forget that pain."

She flicks her hand like she's brushing dust off her sleeve.

"You're in love with her. So go. Be with her. I don't care. Not anymore."

Her voice gets softer, deadlier.

"I only cared because I wanted to survive. But I've already solved that problem."

"No—" I start, but she cuts me off, looking around the room.

"Now," she says, arms crossed tight across her chest, "I want to leave. Am I still exiled and supposed to go back to the forest, or am I free to move wherever I want?" Her voice is deceptively calm.

A growl rips from my throat, low and dark. "You're not going anywhere."

She opens her mouth — probably to argue — but I cut her off before she can chip away at my last thread of sanity.

"I'm the King of Alphas. The ruler of all shifters." I take a step closer, voice dipping. "You're a shifter. Ergo, you follow my command. And I command that you stay right here."

Her eyes bulge. Her mouth falls open.

I take another step forward, towering over her. She barely reaches my shoulder. She has to tilt her head all the way back to look at me. She tries to retreat, to put space between us — but I stop her with a hand curling behind her neck. Not tight. But enough to grab her full attention and make her listen.

"I'm going to figure out what the fuck happened to our bond," I say, each word laced with steel. "And I'm going to win you back. No matter what it takes."

Fire ignites in her gaze. She steps into me, fury pouring off her in waves.

"You're insane," she snaps. "Whatever magic's tangled in you probably took your sanity with it. I will never accept you as my mate again. Never!"

Her eyes narrow to slits, voice like venom.

"I seem to recall you saying that even if you had a mate, it wouldn't be someone as pathetic as me. That I was too weak for someone like you. Worthless. Well guess what, Your Majesty — take those words and shove them so far up your royal ass they never come out!"

I chuckle — low, broken.

"I would never have rejected my mate," I say, softer now. "You could've been human. Magicless. Anything. And I still would've wanted you. You think I didn't bleed when the Priestess looked into my soul and told me there was nothing there? That I was destined to be alone? You think I didn't carry that wound with me every day?"

I shake my head, voice rough. "The night in the ballroom... I was angry. I said those things to hurt you. Because I thought you were trying to hurt me, to slice into that wound even further. I couldn't feel the bond. I didn't know. If I had..."

I swallow.

"If I had, I would have dropped to my knees."

She doesn't soften.

"It doesn't matter now," she says, her voice final. "I don't feel the bond anymore. It's gone."

Her gaze locks with mine.

"I'm not your mate anymore."

"I'm not giving up," I tell her, voice firm. "And you're not going anywhere. I'll fix this."

She huffs, annoyed as hell.

"I may not be able to defy the King's command," she snaps, "but I can set my own conditions."

Her eyes narrow into slits.

"Can't I, *Your Majesty*?"

"You can," I bite back, "if you stop calling me that. My name is Draven."

She smiles — slow, sugar-sweet. And full of venom. "I prefer your title. It would make me happy to keep using it."

Fuck, she's good at this. No shifter can resist pleasing their mate. Especially a lycan.

The word grinds out of me before I can stop it. "Fine."

Her smile stretches. Victory in lace.

"Good. Now take your hand off me. I don't like it."

My fingers drop from the back of her neck instantly. Too fast. Damn it.

Her eyes widen for a second — surprised. Then something sharper slips into them. Calculation. A scheming gleam that makes dread claw up my spine.

"It would make me very happy," she says suddenly, voice bright and innocent, "if you let me leave."

The growl tears from my chest before I even register it. An enraged roar.

The walls tremble. The air warps with magic.

She stumbles back two steps, but I'm already there, closing the distance in a blink.

"Don't talk about leaving again," I snarl, voice vibrating with barely leashed rage.

"Okay, okay! Damn it — freaking lycans!" She throws her hands up, then drags one through her hair, pacing fast. "Fine. I want my own room. A big one. Far away from yours. In another wing of the palace, actually. And access to the palace library."

She turns, finger stabbing the air like a declaration of war.

"That includes the restricted scrolls and manuscripts. And I want to speak to the High Priestess."

She crosses her arms, chin tilted high.

"Those are my conditions."

I nod once. Silent.

She's plotting something — I can see it ticking behind her eyes.

She clearly just made a plan inside that beautiful head of hers to get away from me somehow.

I just need my plan to be better.

CHAPTER 4

Kassira

The moment we step out of Draven's bedroom, we stop dead.

The hallway is packed. Wall to wall with soldiers — all armed, tense, eyes darting between me and the man at my side like they're waiting for another explosion. One wrong move, and this corridor turns into a battlefield.

Standing at the front, just a few feet from the door, is a tall, dark-haired man with eerie green eyes and a death grip on the hilt of a massive sword strapped to his hip. His magic buzzes faintly in the air. Dangerous. On edge.

I've seen him before. Once in the royal town. And again at that cursed ballroom.

Draven's Beta.

"Drev," the man says slowly, voice calm but tight. "You good?" His gaze flicks over me, then settles on Draven again — calculating, alert.

"Take your hand off the sword, Sin," Draven sighs. "I'm back. Mostly." His voice carries the edge of a threat — and something bitter. "Good thing you guys managed to protect my mate, huh?"

The sarcasm is a dagger wrapped in velvet.

Sin straightens immediately, spine snapping into perfect posture as outrage flashes across his face. "From an ancient lycan beast with dragon wings and giant talons?" He throws his hands in the air. "We're lucky you didn't turn us all into pastrami!"

His eyes sharpen with curiosity. "Seriously, what the hell was that? Since when can you shift? And not just any shift — a goddamn ancient lycan?!"

He doesn't wait for an answer. Instead, he tilts his head and looks at me with a crooked smile that would probably charm most women.

"Apologies, beautiful." Draven growls low in warning — I knew it was coming — but Sin ignores him entirely. "We really couldn't get to you. Thirty men in the med bay right now thanks to our fearless king here," he says, thumbing toward Draven. "And they'll be out for days. That's saying something, considering how fast wolves usually heal."

"I like this one," Neris purrs inside my head.

"I do, too," I admit.

"It's fine," I tell Sin. "No apology needed. I handled it."

He flashes a grin. "Clearly. So you really are his mate? That wasn't just a stunt at the party?"

My smile drops.

My eyes narrow. "I don't like you anymore."

Neris snorts and flips her metaphorical tail.

Sin raises an eyebrow, grinning wider. "You liked me?"

Another growl from Draven. Lower. Sharper.

"Enough," he snaps. "Yes, Kassira is my mate—"

"No, I'm not," I cut in, loud and clear.

The hallway goes still. Sharp gasps echo through the crowd. Murmurs ripple like thunder.

Draven's jaw clenches so tight I hear the grind of his teeth.

"That," he growls, "is not up for debate."

He doesn't give me a chance to argue. Just starts marching down the hall.

"To my office. We're finalizing your… conditions." His tone is pure steel. "Sin, you're coming too."

Great. Now we're making it official.

We've been in Draven's office for a few minutes now. He's pacing in front of the desk, updating Sin about the collar wrapped around his lycan — casually — like it's just another item on the royal agenda. They keep asking me questions: What did it look like? What kind of markings did it have? What did the magic feel like?

I answer, but my mind's already working three steps ahead.

If I can't leave, then I'm going to do what I do best — research. It's my secret power. My only power. I'll bury myself in scrolls, books, forbidden texts, whatever it takes to uncover what that leash is, how it works, and most importantly, who the hell put it there. Because that kind of magic isn't just dangerous — it's apocalyptic. Having the King of Alphas — who, by the way, shifts into a winged, indestructible lycan — on a magical leash? That's a disaster waiting to happen. And when that leash gets yanked by some hidden puppet master, who is going to pay the price?

Exactly. All shifters. Including me, because I'm one of them and this idiot rules us all.

I can't build a quiet life anywhere if the king can be unleashed on a murderous rampage on a whim.

Also — minor detail — I need to find a way to sever the bond on his end too. Because if I don't, I'll never be free of Draxis. That lycan will never let me go. They're notorious for their possessiveness. And there has to be something in the royal library. There's always a dusty manuscript for every kind of magical problem.

Too bad I can't blame all this on his perfect little girlfriend. Wouldn't that be satisfying? But even if she's got some power, I know she's a shifter. That kind of magic — the old, deep, twisted kind — could only come from a pure-blooded witch. And yes, I'm bitter about her. So what? I'm bitter about Draven, too! He can go suck a lemon! Or twelve. Both of them!

And speaking of witches — because the universe has excellent comedic timing — the door swings open.

And there she is.

Amira.

Red hair trailing behind her like silk. Gown perfectly tailored. Face flawless. Why couldn't she just be ugly?

"Ven, baby," she coos, voice high and sugary. It makes my molars itch. Makes me stabby.

Draven doesn't even get a full second to react before she's across the room and on him, lips crashing to his like he's the air she's breathing. Her hands on his chest. His hand automatically curves around her waist. Clearly old muscle memory. Familiar territory.

The bond is gone for me and still, the scene cuts deep. It hurts. Not like the physical pain of the bond, but somewhere in my heart. A hollowing-out kind of ache.

Sin gasps audibly beside me.

"*Asshole,*" Neris mutters inside my head.

"*I know,*" I whisper back to her. "*So disrespectful. I get that I severed the bond, but still. Wait five freaking minutes, you—*"

I don't get to finish the thought.

Because suddenly, Draven growls. Low. Furious.

And in the next breath, he shoves Amira off him with enough force to make the entire room freeze. She stumbles back hard, heels slipping, and slams into the wall with a startled gasp.

The silence that follows is delicious.

Sin chuckles.

I glance sideways at him, one eyebrow raised.

He grins, unbothered. Shrugs like this is the most entertaining thing he's seen in months.

I think I like him again.

"Baby, what are you doing?" Amira whines, voice pitched so high it scratches at my eardrums. "I was so worried. I don't understand what happened. And you didn't even come to me — you came here?"

I roll my eyes so hard I nearly see my past lives.

He's a king, sweetheart. Not your emotional support puppy. He has more important stuff to deal with than your drama. How the hell is she making this all about herself?

"Why did you push me, Ven?" Her voice shakes now, wobbly and tear-soaked. Oh, she's dialing it up. Neris huffs inside my head, deeply unimpressed.

Draven doesn't answer her. He's too busy trying to breathe through his obvious meltdown. His chest rises in uneven bursts, jaw locked, one hand pressed tightly against his chest.

"Amira. Leave." His voice finally scrapes out, rough and deadly.

She gasps like he slapped her. "Wh-what?"

His finger lifts — shaking slightly — as he points directly at me.

I blink. Sit up straighter. The whole room shifts to stare. I'm in the spotlight.

"Kassira," he growls, each syllable jagged and rough. "She is my mate. You don't get to touch me anymore. Not like that. Not ever again." His voice trembles with control, thick with a dangerous undertone. "We'll talk later. You need to leave. Now."

I turn to Amira, sugar-sweet smile plastered on my face. I give her a little wave, just to twist the knife.

"Hi." My voice drips honey and sarcasm. "I'm not actually his mate. Well… not anymore. I was. But he's all yours now. Free as a bird."

It's fake as hell. I know it. She knows it. And I don't care. I may not feel the bond anymore. I may not want him. But stars help me, I can't stand her.

The air shifts.

And then the room explodes.

Draven roars. The sound hits the walls and cracks them. The chandelier above us swings violently, glass chiming like warning bells.

Sin grabs his sword.

Draven's wings snap out from behind him, black and wide and massive, tearing through the ceiling. Small pieces of debris rain down around us.

Shit. Too big. Those wings are way too big for this room.

"You *are* my mate," he snarls — and his voice is wrong. Twisted. Echoing. More beast than man.

His eyes are molten silver. No pupils. Something black swirling in the blinding silver. His fangs push past his lips, drawing blood at the corners of his mouth. His hands — gods, his hands — are cracking into the desk now, talons slicing clean through the wood. He's going to have to replace that.

My breath catches.

Neris stirs, disturbingly delighted. *"What do you think it'd look like if he plunged those talons straight into her chest?"* she muses, voice dreamy.

"Bloodthirsty minx," I mutter back, without looking away from the monster in front of me.

"Whatever you say, big guy," I whisper carefully. I can't make him angrier now, he'll swallow us all in one gulp. My voice is low, soothing. My heart is a drum. "Now take a deep breath. Go back inside. Everything's fine."

He doesn't blink. Just stares. Locked on me.

But finally — slowly — his body begins to shift back.

The wings fold inward, muscle trembling. The fangs disappear. The silver bleeds back into ice blue. The claws retract, leaving deep cracks across the desk.

He inhales once. Deep. Centering.

Then he turns.

Amira is frozen. Jaw slack. Eyes wide.

"Leave," he says, voice low but final. Still laced with feral echoes.

She doesn't argue.

She spins around, red hair whipping over her shoulder, and vanishes through the door like she's been lit on fire.

If only it were that easy for me to get the 'leave' command.

"That!" I jab a finger at Draven, heat flaring in my chest. "That was very dramatic! You need to start training that lycan of yours before he tears down the entire palace!"

He exhales and drags a hand down his face, slow and tired. "That would be great... if I could actually feel him. Or talk to him."

Sin leans back in his chair, arms crossed, expression thoughtful now that no one's growling or sprouting claws.

"Drev, I think he only responds to Kassira. To his mate," Sin says, motioning toward me with a casual flick of his fingers. "If she's the key to coaxing him out without triggering a massacre, then maybe start there. Controlled environment. Focused exposure. She clearly has some influence over him. He listens to her. We build from that."

I cross my arms, pretending I'm not flattered that I can tame a rage-fueled monster with a single word. Whatever.

Draven turns his eyes to me again. There's guilt spreading in them like fog.

"I'm sorry about Amira," he says softly. "I don't know what that was. I didn't want to kiss her, I swear. It won't happen again. I'll talk to her. Make everything clear."

I hum under my breath. "I doubt it."

His jaw twitches.

Of course he heard me. Of course they both did. Shifter hearing is just the worst sometimes. I roll my eyes. "Doesn't matter," I mutter, waving the entire conversation away like smoke.

"I'm not in the mood for your woman drama," I say and then point toward Sin. "He's right about the lycan."

I push up from the chair and pace toward the window, thoughts swirling inside my mind. "You should know your beast isn't just an ancient lycan — the kind that hasn't been seen in millennia." I turn and face them again, lifting a brow.

"Sure, the wings are the obvious weird part. Like, who's ever heard of a lycan with wings? Ok, you already had the wings so we could overlook that. But that's not all." I start counting off on my fingers. "The talons? Full-on dragon. Not shifter claws. Dragon. The fangs are too big — he can't even close his mouth properly. And when I was inspecting the collar under his fur..." I pause. For the drama. "I saw scales. Dragon scales."

Both men blink at me like I just slapped them with a dead fish.

"So yeah," I finish, clapping my hands once, loud. "Congratulations. You've got yourself a weird-ass hybrid ancient lycan. A flying, fanged, scaled murder machine. Have fun figuring that out."

They're still staring at me, so I clap again — louder. "Now! I want to go to my room. A nice one. With a door that locks from the inside. And I expect full access to the palace library, as I was promised." I narrow my eyes. "Including the restricted section."

They both nod.

Good. Because I may be stuck here... but I'm going to dig into every scroll and spell this palace owns until I find my way out of this place.

CHAPTER 5

Draven

Ever since Amira and I agreed to the arranged mating, things ran smoothly between us. We worked well together. She adapted quickly — to palace life, to royal protocol, to the rhythm of power. She learned fast. Played the part even faster.

She's from Mirenwulf — one of the six Prime Packs. Her bloodline is pure strength, top-tier shifter lineage. Her father's the Alpha Prime there. Her uncle's one of my most trusted advisors. And one of her brothers is on track to becoming Head Warrior if he keeps grinding the way he does.

After I secured my throne — no challengers left standing, no question about who the King was — my Council started pressing me to consider an arranged mating. I thought I had no mate. The High Priestess found no Mate Spark in me. So I listened.

Every pack needs a Luna. The Royal Pack is no exception. I needed someone strong. Mateless. Politically sound. Capable of earning the loyalty of alphas across the realm.

And over a year ago, I made my choice.

Amira.

Her true mate had died. Her family was loyal. Her presence — poised, strong, confident. She checked every box the Council put in front of me. When they presented her as an option, I just said yes. I wanted to be done with the search.

We agreed on a two-year courtship. Time to get to know each other. Appear united in the eyes of the public. Time for her to learn everything about what it means to be Queen.

I was supposed to mark her in just a few months.

The thought makes bile rise in my throat.

She didn't want to wait the full two years. The Council didn't either. They pushed. Pressed. Urged. But I insisted.

Now, looking back, I think it was the lycan. Pushing against the magic choking us both. Screaming that our mate was still out there. Fighting for her, even when I couldn't hear him.

I'm only grateful he was strong enough to hold the line.

Amira's father will lose his damn mind over this situation. Tough shit.

My mate is more important than anything.

"Amira," I say, resting my forearms on the cracked desk between us, "things are very simple now. Our arrangement is over."

Her brows knit together, but I press on before she can interrupt.

"I found my true mate. And the moment I did, our arranged mating was dissolved."

I lean in slightly, meeting her gaze without flinching. "I'm sorry," I add. "Not about finding my true mate, of course. But I know how much time you've invested preparing to take on the Luna role. Studying the royal bloodline. Memorizing history, protocol, causes. You worked hard."

Her breath shudders. Her voice is small, shaky. "I... I don't understand," she says, eyes filling with tears. "I thought you didn't have a mate. Like me. I thought we were building something real."

She hesitates, then whispers, "I fell in love with you, Ven. Don't you care about me? At all?"

Her eyes lock on mine, shining with hurt, and for a moment — a very brief moment — guilt stirs in my chest. Not because I wronged her. I didn't. But because somewhere along the way, she clearly convinced herself I was something I never promised to be. But it slightly pisses me off, too.

I exhale through my nose. "Amira," I say, keeping my voice calm, "you knew the terms from the beginning. This was a political alliance. I told you clearly I couldn't offer love. I never misled you."

She flinches slightly. My words hit, but I won't apologize for them. I'm not being cruel, I'm just honest.

"I didn't need your love," she says suddenly, louder.

Stronger. "I gave you mine anyway." Her palm slams against her chest. "And I'm ready to serve. I know what it means to be Luna of the Royal Pack. I've trained for it. I've earned it."

Her voice breaks again. "Can she even do it?" she whispers. "Can she stand beside you in the eyes of all the Prime Packs? Of the world? Does she even want you?"

That one lands. Hard.

But not enough to shake me.

I've spent years believing I didn't have a mate. I hardened myself around that truth. And now — when I thought it would never happen — I've been given something sacred. My soul's match. My other half. She may not want me right now. But that doesn't matter.

Because I will earn her back. She will always be mine.

I square my shoulders. My tone turns cold.

"It's done, Amira. And I won't have you speaking of my mate like that again."

She blinks at me, stunned.

"I understand this hurts. I do. But questioning her place beside me? That's a line you don't cross. Not if you want to leave this palace with your dignity intact."

I pause, let the words settle.

"I've already sent word to your father," I finish. "You'll be returning to Mirenwulf tomorrow."

I sigh and push up from the desk.

Amira's still sitting there, eyes wide and glassy. Full of

tears.

"I'm sure you understand why you need to return to your pack," I say, keeping my voice even. It sucks for her, I know. But I can't have a woman I slept with and presented as my chosen Luna to the public anywhere near my true mate. It will hurt Kassira and I won't allow that.

Amira rises slowly from the chair, head bowed. Her voice is a whisper. "It's not fair."

She lifts her gaze, chin trembling. "I wish I'd known that was our last kiss."

Hell, this is stretching too long.

"You'll be fine, Amira," I tell her, voice clipped. "You're strong enough to get through this."

She takes a step toward me, hand lifting — a reflex, maybe. Or a willing mistake.

A warning growl rolls out of me before I can stop it.

She gasps and goes still, arm frozen mid-air.

"What the hell do you think you're doing?" My voice drops to a snarl. "You know better. You don't touch a shifter after he's found his mate." My eyes narrow on her. "You barely made it out alive earlier. And that was because I knew you didn't have all the facts yet."

"I'm sorry," she breathes. "I didn't think. I just wanted to hug you. Just once more."

She steps back. Two paces. Hands up. Retreating.

"I'll go now," she whispers. "Goodbye, Ven."

I don't answer.

My eyes stay locked on the door long after it closes.

This whole leash situation is eating at my instincts. Making me suspicious of everyone. Paranoid. The kind of ancient magic that can cage a creature like Draxis? That takes a pure-blooded witch — not just power, but heritage.

And if I didn't know, with absolute certainty, that Amira is a shifter... she'd be on my list. Right near the top.

Out of all the possible reasons for someone to collar me, one stands out above the rest.

Power.

My bloodline has always ruled the Royal Pack. Always gave the Alpha King. Always. Anyone could challenge us, and they did, but no one ever won.

So yeah — if someone wanted access to absolute power over all shifters... leashing me would be the obvious move. And Amira got closer to that power than most.

I step into the royal library without a sound.

I already know where she is — I can feel it. A constant, aching pull in my chest leads me to her without fail. A bond that should be gone, but still hums beneath my skin, alive and wild.

She's at one of the large oak tables, surrounded by

towers of ancient books and crumbling scrolls. Her face is bent in concentration, a small furrow between her brows, fingers stained faintly with ink. She looks like she always belonged here — fierce and untouchable.

"What do you want, Your Majesty?" she says without looking up.

Fuck, even her voice is sharp enough to cut.

"I brought you something to eat." I set the plate down beside her carefully — pastries, sliced fruit, tiny sandwiches. "You've been locked in here for hours. You didn't eat."

Finally, she looks at me. Suspicious eyes. Arms crossed. Defensive posture engaged.

"Keeping tabs on my movements?" she asks flatly.

I smile, because of course she'd say that. "Obviously. If you insist on going through half the restricted archives in a single sitting, someone has to make sure you don't collapse face-first into old and dusty paper."

She sniffs the food once. Her stomach audibly growls, and she huffs, annoyed at herself.

"That smells... unfairly good," she mutters, reaching out — then stopping mid-reach to narrow her eyes at me.

"This is not me accepting a mate offering," she says sternly. "Got it?"

"Crystal clear," I reply, nodding. Still smiling. But when she finally takes a bite of the sandwich, something warm unfurls in my chest. I almost release a contented growl, instinct tugging at me, but I clamp it down just in time.

I take the seat next to her and grab one of the books, flipping it open like I actually intend to read it. Truth is, I'm watching her. Everything about her is fascinating. She's a beautiful contradiction. Someone who seems powerless at first glance, but she's actually stronger than any warrior I've met. None of them would have survived the pain of a rejection for six months and still have their sanity by the end.

"How's your little girlfriend?" she mumbles around a bite. "Still upset?"

My jaw tightens at the memory. Amira's last stunt was too much — reaching for me after everything I told her.

"She's not my girlfriend," I say, voice low. "She'll be leaving for her father's pack tomorrow."

Kassira's eyebrows shoot up. "Seriously?" There's too much glee in her voice for someone pretending not to care. "How'd she take it? Did she cry? Beg? Throw something at you?"

I grin despite myself. "It went about as well as you'd expect—"

I stop. My eyes catch on something in the book I've been pretending to read. A paragraph, just a few words.

She leans forward, chewing slower now. "Why'd you stop?"

My blood goes cold.

I turn the book toward her and tap the line that stopped me cold. "This — right here. It says controlling magic can only be placed on a lycan when they're at their most vulnerable. Tiny windows of time. As a newborn... or during deep grief." I glance up, voice low. "The collar — it's definitely controlling magic. It's controlling my lycan and my part of the bond."

"And your mind, most likely," Kassira murmurs. Her voice is soft, but the words hit hard. She meets my eyes. "You never shifted because of it. That collar stopped everything. You should've turned at ten, when all lycans do. Which means someone got to you before then." She leans back, fingers tapping against the wood. Then throws her head back, groaning. "Ugh, I really, really wanted it to be your little girlfriend. But even if she were a pure-blood witch, she would've been too young back then." She huffs. "This would've been so much simpler if it was her."

I bite down a curse. "Yeah," I mutter. "I thought about that too."

Her head snaps toward me, a spark in her eyes. "Oh? You've had bad thoughts about the love of your life?"

I frown. "She's not the love of my life," I say flatly. "I never loved her. It was an arranged mating. A political alliance. The pack needed a Luna, my Council insisted and I thought I was mateless."

Kassira's jaw drops slightly. Her expression is all disbelief. "Uh-huh. Didn't look like just politics when you two were playing lovebirds in public."

I sigh. "It was for appearances. For the packs. Strong image. Strong unity."

She squints at me, lips pursed like she's trying to decide what to throw something at my head. "And what about her true mate? You can't just reject a mate bond for status. That's illegal."

"He died," I say simply. "Years ago. The Council vetted her, and she was their top pick. She knew the role. I agreed. There were no more challenges for the throne, I had stability. It made sense."

She groans and drags a hand down her face. "You always have an answer for everything, don't you?"

I grin and lean back in my chair. "I sure do, gorgeous."

I slide the plate of pastries closer to her, throwing in a wink for good measure. "Eat. They're delicious. Just like you."

She blinks. Once. Twice. Then lets out a sharp, incredulous laugh. "Wait. Wait — were you just trying to flirt with me?"

I narrow my eyes, lips curving. "Maybe… Is it working?"

She snorts. "You're terrible at it! Seriously. How can you be this bad at flirting?"

I cross my arms, wounded. "I never had to flirt," I mumble. "Like you can do it better."

She smirks while she picks up a pastry, eyes locked on mine, and takes a slow, sultry bite. Her lids lower. A soft sound escapes her. "Mmm," she purrs, licking her lips, "you were right, Your Majesty. This pastry really is soooo, so delicious."

My mouth is dry. I'm leaning in before I realize I've moved. "It is?" I breathe.

She pops the rest of the pastry in her mouth and grins. "Sure is!" Cheerful. Absolutely evil.

I blink, trying to bring my brain back. What just happened?

I clear my throat and sit straighter, oddly disappointed. "Right. Okay. Focus." I rub a hand over my jaw. "I called for the High Priestess. She'll arrive in a week."

Kassira nods, eyes serious again. "Good. We need answers. Whoever did this — whoever put that leash on you — they're patient. But if Draxis broke through, that means the collar's weakening. And whoever's behind it... they'll feel the pressure. They'll act soon."

"I agree. That's why Sin and I already set up a perimeter in the West Forest. Border of the palace lands. I want to try bringing Draxis out in a controlled space. If you're okay with it, I'd like to start tomorrow."

She tilts her head, thinking, then nods once. "Okay."

Then she glances at the half-full plate, smirking. "I'd like more pastries. And a steak sandwich."

I'm on my feet before she finishes the sentence. "I'll be right back."

CHAPTER 6

Kassira

I wake up early. Bright-eyed. Clear-headed. For the first time in months, I feel like I actually slept. Like all the pieces inside of me have finally stopped rattling.

Two days since I severed the bond. Two whole days.

I still can't believe just yesterday morning I woke up in this gilded, over-polished, too-lavish palace... with a massive lycan drooling next to me.

"*I could get used to these expensive sheets and such a big, soft bed,*" Neris sighs dreamily.

"*Same,*" I murmur, stretching like a cat. "*And the food? Stars, don't even get me started.*"

I get ready for the day and walk to the door, humming under my breath.

I swing it open, only to have a giant idiot king come crashing in.

Literally.

Half of his massive body tumbles through the doorway, slamming flat on the floor at my feet. The back of his head smacks the stone. Hard. His eyes snap open like he's been sucker-punched by the goddess herself.

I blink. He blinks. We just... blink at each other.

"What the hell are you doing?" I demand, staring down at him like he's lost what little of his brain he had left.

He's on his feet in an instant, rubbing the embarrassment off his face. His hair's a mess. Eyes a little wild. He shakes his head a few times.

"Hello?" I snap, stepping forward. "I said I wanted my room far from yours. You remember that part of my terms, right? The 'away from you' part? Sleeping in front of my door was definitely not what I meant!"

He doesn't answer.

His keeps his hands pressed over his face and then I hear him whisper.

"I forgot you."

I freeze.

"What?"

He looks up. And gods — his expression is wrecked. Haunted. Something about it twists painfully inside my chest before I can stop it.

"I forgot you," he says again, voice strained. "Last night... I woke up from something. A dream. A nightmare. I don't know. I felt the bond pulling at me and I didn't know why. I didn't even remember who you were."

My breath catches. He keeps going.

"Just like before," he says quietly. "I didn't remember you were my mate. Not until I followed the pull of the bond and arrived in front of your door."

He presses a hand to his throat. "So I stayed. I didn't want to forget you again."

"I think the magic's getting worse," he adds. "If I spend too much time away from you, it becomes stronger."

"That's… disturbing," I whisper.

Inside my head, Neris growls. *"Let Draxis out. Let him chew at that leash until it snaps."*

"You're right," I murmur to her.

I lift my chin and look at Draven.

"We need to try and bring Draxis out. This morning. Now."

His brows lift slightly. I press forward.

"We're not wasting time. We bring Draxis out today and every day until it gets easier. Until that leash breaks. My wolf thinks he's the answer. I do, too."

He studies me for a moment. Then nods once, slowly.

"I think you might be right."

I scowl at Draven's stupidly handsome face.

He just smiles at me.

We're deep in the West Forest, not far from the palace. It's the perfect place for this little disaster waiting to happen. Isolated. Warded. Reinforced with spell-etched stone and layered with royal-level shielding runes. If Draxis loses control in here, he can't hurt anyone.

Except maybe me. And Sin.

Sin's the only one here besides us. Because no one else knows about the leash. Everyone else just thinks Draven is a late bloomer with an ancient lycan form. Very late. Very dramatic.

Draven refused to tell anyone. He's completely paranoid. He made a whole list of suspects and slapped everyone on it. His Council. The Alpha Primes. His Gamma. Every coven of witches in the world. Even Amira. Just in case. I hate how much I liked that.

"Come on, Your Royal Pain in the Ass," I snap, hands on my hips. "Focus. You know how to call your wings. Same thing — but this time, call the lycan."

He sighs deeply, like I've just asked him to solve the meaning of life. "We've been at this for over an hour. I've tried. Repeatedly. Nothing." He flings his hands up and starts pacing, all frustration and tension. "What even brought him forward last time? The sever—" He cuts himself off, jaw clenching. A growl vibrates from his chest. "That can't happen again. Ever."

I blink. Oh. Maybe he's onto something.

I take a couple steps back, turn to the side and lift my voice. "I'm leaving! Do you hear me, Draxis? I'm walking out of this forest, out of this palace—"

Draven turns his head, brows drawing together. "You're lying. I can hear it in your voice."

Sin strolls closer, arms crossed. "This is painful. You're both idiots. Figures you're soulmates."

That's it! My eyes widen. I spin to face Draven directly.

"I am not your mate!" I shout at Draven. "You hear me, Draxis? I am not your mate!"

Draven growls right on cue, eyes flashing silver. Oh. Oh, this might actually work.

"I am not your mate, Draxis," I repeat sweetly, sing-song. "Never will be again."

He straightens. Smiles like he knows a secret. "That was a lie," he says, smug. "I could feel it. You don't believe that."

"Yes, I do!" I shoot back, heat rising in my face. *Neris? Back me up here.*

There's a long pause. Then my wolf sighs.

"Well... there were some very plausible explanations..." she mumbles.

"Neris!" I bark at her with my inside voice. *"Take it back! We are not falling! We have a plan. Fix the leash. Sever the bond on his end. Leave. That's the mission."*

She huffs. *"I know. But... he was under a spell. He didn't reject us by choice. And if there's even the smallest chance we could be with our true mate... is that really such a terrible thing?"*

"*I will chew your tail off, wolf,*" I threaten. "*You just want to control a massive murder monster and make him maul people for you.*"

"*I also want our mate,*" she says softly. "*He's our twin soul, Kass. The only one we'll ever get. Even if the bond's severed, our souls are still connected. Born together, from the same Spark. Meant to find each other. I'm not saying jump into his arms today. But maybe we don't slam the door shut, either.*"

She pauses. Then adds sweetly, "*We can still torture him some more. That is fun.*"

I sigh. Dammit. Of course my wolf would fold like a piece of paper. It only took her a day and a half. She got her explanations, it all made sense and now she wants her lycan.

Typical wolf behavior.

I get it. I do. True mates are sacred in our world. Twin souls that complete each other perfectly. No one else can touch that kind of happiness — that kind of peace. And sure, some shifters, very few, still accept the punishment and reject it. Assholes with no heart or too much pride. I thought Draven was one of them.

I look at the culprit, who is currently giving me a smug, stupid smile.

I do not have time for this.

First we remove the leash. Then we see if I need to leash my own wolf before she starts howling love songs under the lycan's window.

The bond is severed — on our side, at least. And there's

no undoing that. Severing is permanent. Final.

As that thought settles, another slams into me — I'm a genius!

I turn to Sin. He looks about as engaged as a corpse. Stifling a yawn.

Perfect.

I grab his face before he can react, palms on both cheeks, drag his head down and plant a big, wet kiss right on his lips.

His eyes go wide and not even a full second later, a thunderous growl rips through the clearing. The ground cracks. Birds flee like the apocalypse just rolled in.

Sin's voice is a dry mutter. "I'll never forgive you if that beast bites my head off."

I step back and grin. "Don't worry, bestie. I won't let him kill you." I pat his cheek. "Just… don't run. He'll chase you down and peel you like a grape."

Sin glares at me. "I won't forget this."

"It'll all be ok," I chirp, then turn.

And there he is.

Draxis.

Massive. Towering. Drenched in shadows and rage. Black fur rippling over slabs of muscle. Wings spread wide enough to eclipse the sun. Silver eyes locked on Sin like he's already dead. Fangs glinting. Talons twitching.

Yeah. He's beautiful.

I move slowly toward him. Careful.

"Hello, Draxis," I say softly. He doesn't look at me. His gaze is still fixed on Sin — but one of his ears twitches at the sound of my voice.

"Look at me, big guy," I coax. "It would make me very happy if you took your eyes off Sin and let him live another day."

He finally shifts his gaze to me. Silver eyes. Burning. Blinking slow. Then — one talon lifts, points at Sin.

"Bleeeeeed," he hisses.

Oh gods.

"Nope," I say, sweet as honey. "No bleeding. No hurting Sin. That would make me very unhappy."

I reach him and lift a hand, pressing my palm to his chest. His fur is warm. Coarse. Alive with energy.

"Is Draven awake?" I ask gently.

He shakes his massive head. "Maaaatttte," he growls, low and deep.

"Yes, yes," I murmur. "That's something we'll need to talk about. Later."

His eyes don't leave mine. Not even for a blink.

"First," I whisper, "we need to find a way to take that collar off you."

He nods once. Deadly. Calm. So intense.

"Tell me something," I say, keeping my voice steady. "Was the magic of the leash weaker the day you first shifted?"

"Yeeessss," Draxis rumbles, the sound slithering out of him.

My heart stutters. Progress.

"And now?" I ask. "Is it repairing itself?"

He nods once — slow, reluctant. Damn.

"Hmm..." I murmur, chewing the inside of my cheek.

"Ask him if he knows who did it," Neris whispers, practically bouncing inside my head. *"Who put the leash on him?"*

I nod subtly. "Draxis," I say, meeting those molten silver eyes, "do you know who put the leash on you?"

His growl deepens instantly, a low, thunderous sound that starts in his chest and rolls through the clearing like war drums.

"Yeeessss," he hisses, fury boiling in his breath.

My eyes snap wide. "Who was it?"

He whines. Low. Gutting.

"You can't tell me?" I ask, gently now.

He nods once, miserable.

"Is the magic stopping you from saying it?"

Another nod. Shit. Of course it is.

"Does it weaken every time you shift?" I press.

"Nnnooo." The sound is rough, broken.

I curse under my breath. There goes our plan. All that build-up, all that hope, and now—

His giant snout bops gently against my forehead.

I blink. "What are you doing?"

"Maaaatttteee," he growl-hisses, then bops me again. Firmer this time.

I frown, completely lost. "What?"

"I think he wants to meet me," Neris says, tail practically wagging through my spine. *"Let me out, Kass. Please?"*

"You want to meet Neris?" I ask Draxis.

He nods so fast it's almost ridiculous, then starts sniffing my face like I'm a delicious buffet. His wings twitch, his whole giant body humming with anticipation.

I turn to Sin. "You can go now! We're good here."

"You don't have to tell me twice!" he shouts, already running toward the palace.

I glance back just in time to see Draxis following Sin's path with narrowed, bloodthirsty eyes.

I grab a fistful of fur and yank.

"Hey! Don't look at him like that! Sin is off-limits. You'll play nice, or no wolf for you."

Draxis whips his head to me, panting like a dog who just heard the word 'treat'. Tongue out. Tail... twitching.

Gods help me, he's adorable. Deadly adorable.

"Okay, fine," I say. "But if you want to meet Neris, you have to cover your eyes."

He tilts his head like he can't understand the words I've just said. I know he can!

"I mean it!" I cross my arms. "Now, Draxis. Cover. Your. Eyes. I'm not shifting with you watching. Not happening."

He lets out a dramatic huff like I'm being unreasonable, but finally lifts one of his massive paws and slaps it over his eyes.

"Thank you," I mutter, already pulling off my clothes. Once I'm bare, I release the shift.

Muscles burn. Skin stretches. My vision fractures — then realigns. And just like that, Neris is in control.

She yips once — joyful, excited — and bolts straight at him.

"Neris! What the hell are you doing?! Be cool!" I shout from inside.

"I'm going to sniff him everywhere!" she says gleefully. *"He smells like fire and death and cuddles!"*

Shit. This is going to be a disaster.

The moment Draxis drops his paw and sees Neris, it's game over.

He lunges, catching her mid-run like she weighs nothing — which, compared to him, she absolutely does — and crashes to the ground, caging her beneath his massive body. His wings curl around them both like a fortress.

Neris looks microscopic under him. But of course, my reckless wolf doesn't care. Her tail starts wagging like she's found her new favorite chew toy. She's nuzzling into his fur, sniffing him aggressively and I have zero control right now. Dammit.

"Maaatttteeee," Draxis growls, shifting slightly to the side to get a better angle. He sniffs her a few times — slowly, big puffs of air — and the little idiot freezes, like she's just remembered he's the size of a cottage and definitely carnivorous.

Then, out of nowhere, his massive tongue swipes across her entire face in one sloppy, gleeful motion.

Draxis growls again, playful this time — a low, rumbling challenge.

Neris bolts.

Yipping. Darting between his legs.

And now they're playing.

Playing.

The world is on fire, we're dealing with a cursed leash and possibly a puppet master with god-tier magic, and my wolf is out here playing 'catch me if you can' with an ancient monster.

Draxis doesn't let her get far. The ground shakes beneath his paws as he lunges forward and scoops her up like a squeaky toy. She's airborne for all of two seconds before he pulls her close to his chest, nuzzling his snout into the curve of her neck with a contented huff.

And of course, they're adorable. Absolutely adorable.

I'm just starting to relax, thinking 'okay, let them have a moment', when I feel it. A shift. A flicker of heat.

A nip.

Right at the base of Neris' neck.

And the traitor — the absolute traitor — tilts her head to the side, baring her throat like an offering.

NO. NO. NOOOO!

"*Neris!*" I yell from inside her mind. "*Absolutely not! You are not letting him mark you!*"

She's not listening. She's floating in a cloud of dumb, mate-drunk bliss.

I shove forward, clawing control, and slam into her body just in time to butt Draxis in the snout with my head. I start thrashing in his hold, contorting my limbs like an angry ferret.

"*Let. Me. Go!*" I snarl.

He growls low, stubborn and feral. "Maaaattttteee."

Shut up, you overgrown lizard-wolf.

I snap my jaw around his forearm and bite. My teeth scream in protest.

Ow. Scales. I forgot about the damn scales.

He sighs. A long, suffering exhale like I've ruined his day. And then — finally — he sets me down.

The second my paws hit the ground, I shift back, human again and pissed off. I jab my finger at the center of his stupid snout.

"Bad lycan. Bad. Bring Draven back. Right. Now."

He rolls his glowing silver eyes at me and growls softly, frustration steaming off him.

"Now, Draxis," I snap. "Don't test me. Let Draven back!"

He lets out another huff, full of drama, and sulks backward. Then the shift begins — fast, fluid, and the next blink reveals Draven, standing in the same spot, gloriously naked and not the least bit apologetic.

His gaze finds mine. He doesn't blink. Doesn't move.

I blink first. Then realize — I'm naked too.

"Turn around, idiot!" I screech, covering myself with my arms.

He smirks, infuriatingly slow, and turns with deliberate movements. Way too slow.

Muttering curses under my breath, I scramble to pull my clothes back on.

This was a terrible idea.

Everything's messier now. More complicated.

I spot a pair of pants and a shirt draped over a branch — Sin must've left them — and I chuck them straight at Draven's stupid, perfect ass.

"Get dressed, Your Majesty," I grumble. "We've accomplished nothing. Your lycan is a stubborn jackass, he gave us more questions than answers, and now I need therapy."

CHAPTER 7

Draven

I'm flat on my back in the West Forest clearing, staring at the sky.

Kassira lies beside me, close enough that I can feel her warmth, her breath. We've been doing this routine for the last three days — drag Draxis out each morning, try to keep him calm, try to learn something. Rinse. Repeat.

Sin helps.

Unfortunately.

The only reason he's still breathing is because Draxis listens to Kass. If he didn't, Sin would've been carved into tiny pieces of steak by now.

Still no progress. I can't reach my lycan. Can't feel him. Can't control him. I'm just… locked out. And every night, I end up camped in front of Kassira's door praying the magic doesn't get even stronger somehow and I end up forgetting her forever. If we weren't shifters — if people didn't understand what a mate bond means — it would probably look weird. Hell, it probably does anyway.

Speaking of things that are weird...

That strange bruise in the center of my chest? Still there. A dark blotch of pain that never fades. It should've healed in seconds. Instead, it's spreading. Deepening. The High Priestess gets here in a few days. She better have answers, because I'm not in the mood to guess whether it's a magical infection, a curse, or a countdown to my fucking death.

I've been watching everyone. Every movement. Every word. Nothing suspicious yet — no tells, no magic scents, no misplaced glances.

In the meantime, I help Kass with her research in the library. Scrolls, grimoires, ancient tomes. Anything we can get our hands on. I try to stay near her as much as possible.

Seven hours.

That's the longest I can be apart from her before the leash starts rotting my brain again. Before I start forgetting that I have a mate.

That panic? It never leaves me.

So I stay close. As close as I can.

And I feed her, too. Constantly. You'd think it's the mate bond making me do it — instinct, hormones, obsession — but it's not. She loves food. Good food makes her happy. And I like watching her be happy. So now, when she's deep in study mode, the cook is under strict orders to go crazy with the most delicious recipes he has. And I bring each one of them to her.

Even Draxis is playing his part — or so she tells me. Apparently, he's taken to hunting for her.

And for Neris, of course.

Yesterday, he dropped three dead deer at her feet in a matter of minutes after shifting. Neris was thrilled. Kass was... not. She's banned her wolf from shifting around Draxis now, ever since that idiot tried to mark her — and Neris nearly let him.

So now they're grounded. No contact. Until Kass says otherwise.

The pain of the broken bond follows me around every second. Twisted and deep, settled in every fiber of my being. I can't help but feel frustrated. Pissed off. Not with Kass, but with the whole situation. Why the fuck did this have to happen to me?

When I find that witch who put the collar on me — who forced me to betray my mate, to hurt her — I'll tear them apart. Slowly.

And then I'll do it again.

A sudden stab of pain slams through my chest. Sharp. Blinding. All my muscles seize.

I grit my teeth and dig my fingers into the dirt.

"Did you accept it immediately?" Kassira asks suddenly. Her voice is quiet, but sharp. Like she's been holding the question in for a long time. "No questions asked?"

I turn my head to look at her. "Accept what?"

She meets my gaze, eyes steady. "What the High

Priestess told you. That you had no Mate Spark. That there was no one meant for you."

I exhale slowly, the memory wrapping cold fingers around my heart. "No," I whisper. "I didn't."

My eyes drift back to the sky, the clouds unmoving. "I still had hope. Even after she told me I was mateless, I held on. Told myself maybe she was wrong. Even if no other Priestess before got it wrong, maybe she was the first one." My voice drops lower. "But then I didn't shift. And that... that broke something in me. Sent me into a spiral. Ate away at my confidence, my pride."

I pause, remembering the way the loneliness used to scream in my ears with every birthday that came and went.

"But I still hoped," I murmur. "Twenty came and went. By then, most shifters already know. Already meet. Already bond. But I still waited. Then twenty-one. Twenty-two. Twenty-four. At twenty-six. That's when I stopped hoping. That's when I agreed to the arranged mating. Told myself it was my duty. Told myself I just had to accept that there really was no mate for me."

I glance at her again. "What about you? You're twenty-six now. What did you think when twenty hit and you still hadn't met your mate?"

She gives a small shrug, but her shoulders are tense. "That I was just... unlucky." Her voice is steady, but I can hear the weight behind it. "Part of me wondered if my mate was dead. That would explain the silence. I kept going to the pack's Priestess, begging her to check my Mate Spark. Make sure that it didn't dull, that it still shone."

She looks down at her hands. "It always did. Bright, she said. Brighter than most. I just had to be patient. She told me my case was rare. But my mate was out there."

Her voice tightens. "I waited for you for so long. And then you rejected me. Sent me into exile. Alone with the pain. Neris, too. We were devastated. Then bitter. And then angry." She sighs. "I understand it now — the collar, the spell, all of it. But the memory is still there."

"I know," I say, voice low. Then I shift, push up on one elbow, eyes fixed on her. "But that doesn't mean I'm giving up. I won't. You're mine, Kassira. And I'll do whatever it takes to earn you back."

She chuckles — soft, almost disbelieving. Like she doesn't want to smile but can't help it. "We have bigger problems to deal with right now."

Her smile fades, and she looks at me again. This time, there's no teasing in her eyes.

"I don't feel the bond anymore, Draven. It's gone. There's no bringing it back. Not ever."

I nod, slowly. "That doesn't matter."

She blinks.

"The bond only tells us who we belong to," I say quietly. "It doesn't make us fall in love. It doesn't choose our happiness. I don't need the bond to know you're it for me. I don't need magic to love you."

Her eyes soften. She stares at me a moment longer, then shakes her head and laughs. "You didn't actually lose that hope, did you?"

She stands and brushes herself off. "Come on. I have a mountain of dusty manuscripts calling my name. Will you help me again today, or do you have kingly duties to pretend to care about?"

I push up to my feet, brushing dirt off my palms. "All royal business is on hold until we cut this damn leash off me."

We're halfway back to the palace when I hear it.

Angry shouting. Flesh meeting flesh. Fangs breaking skin. Blood hitting the dirt.

The training field.

"Wait here," I tell Kassira, already breaking into a run before she can object.

I sprint toward the noise, following the scent of adrenaline and blood. Two warriors are locked in the center of the field, fists flying, claws out. No one else in sight. Just them. No trainer. No witnesses. No control.

Ervin and Levi.

I know them both. Ervin — cocky, skilled, but too arrogant to ever be trusted with a command. And Levi... Amira's younger brother.

"Stop!" I shout, layering my voice with Alpha command.

They freeze mid-blow. Bloodied. Panting. Eyes wide.

"What the hell is going on?" I demand, stalking toward them.

They both bow their heads in submission, shoulders rigid.

Levi speaks first. "I apologize, Alpha. He insulted my family. I lost control."

I shift my attention to Ervin and lace my next words with more power. "What did you say?"

Ervin flinches. The truth tumbles out, clenched between his teeth. "I asked him if he slept his way to the top, just like his sister. I'm sorry, Alpha."

My jaw locks. Fury burns through me like wildfire.

"You're doing two hundred perimeter laps. Starting now. And you're on cleaning duty for the next month. You keep running your mouth like that, and I'll cut you from the warrior program myself. I need soldiers, not gossiping, arrogant brats. Move."

Ervin takes off without another word, boots thudding against the ground.

I turn to Levi. "Are you alright?"

"Yes, Alpha," he says, still not meeting my eyes.

"You can go," I tell him. "If anyone else gives you trouble, come straight to me."

He nods and takes a small step forward. "I can handle myself." Then, voice lower, almost hesitant: "I'm glad you found your true mate, Alpha."

There's something about the way he says it. Not just the words — the weight behind them. No bitterness. No resentment. Just... relief.

Then he turns and walks away.

Strange.

I watch him go, jaw tight, thoughts turning. Why would he sound relieved Amira won't be Luna?

"Did you hear that?" I ask, not bothering to turn around. Because of course she didn't listen and stay put.

"No, what'd he say?" Kassira asks, coming to stand beside me.

"It was the way he said it," I mutter. "Like he was... grateful. Like he didn't want his sister to be Luna."

She shrugs. "Could be sibling rivalry."

"Maybe," I say, frowning as I stare after him. I'll keep an eye on Levi.

Suddenly, a jolt of warmth and sparks shoots up my arm.

I look down to find Kassira's hand in mine.

She tugs. "Come on, Your Majesty. We've got work to do. And I'm starving."

I blink. She's touching me. Willingly.

And just like that, a ridiculous smile breaks all over my face.

CHAPTER 8

Kassira

Excerpt from the diary of the High Priestess Marilla DeVohn - 300 years old manuscript

"It is commonly taught — in schools and village firesides alike — that modern lycans descend directly from the ancient ones. Towering beasts of shadow and fury, primal ancestors whose blood birthed the packs of today. This, however, is a carefully constructed lie.

In truth, there were never such things as 'ancient lycans.' The creatures referenced in myth were never lycans at all. They were something else entirely.

They were called Hellhounds. Monsters with wings of smoke and talons carved from flame.

Not bound to the Moon. Not blessed by the gods. Not tied even to the lord of the Underworld. These were entities outside of the natural order, born not of wombs or stars, but of hellfire and death. Demigods in their own right. There were seven in total, walking the Earth more than two thousand years ago. Indestructible. Without mercy.

They sought only one thing, the only thing they were missing: a soul. A Spark. That elusive glimmer of purpose the gods gave freely to lesser beings. They wanted to bring light to the dark, hollow void inside them. They wanted the Mate Spark — the soul's twin flame. And they were willing to tear the heavens apart to get it.

The gods tried to stop them. With weapons. With strategy. With prophecy. But nothing worked. You cannot strategize against chaos. You cannot outmaneuver something that has no rules.

So the Hellhounds, through relentless destruction, arrived at the steps of the heavens and won the war. They made the gods bow to them. The Moon Goddess was the first to accept their victory. But she also understood their pain. In the end, she was the only god who accepted their request and when they finally gained their Sparks — when they met the mates tethered to their own souls — they quieted. They retreated. They became protectors, not destroyers.

It is said that each bonded pair tamed the storm within the other. And together, they created the first packs of lycans and dragons. The original seven. As gratitude toward the Moon for her gift, they also took her wolves under their protection.

Since then, only a diluted drop of their blood has lingered in certain shifter lines. Harmless and dormant.

The High Priestesses of the Moon have protected this

knowledge for millennia at the request of our goddess. The rest of the gods weaved the legends of the ancient lycans and, in their stories, stripped the Hellhounds of their wings and their talons and the scales under their fur. Because they didn't want the world to remember the only time in history when they had to kneel.

The resurgence of a true Hellhound — full-blooded and awakened — is an omen we all need to fear. It will either come to destroy the world or save it. But the world won't know until the last moment.

A final note of warning: the bond of a Hellhound cannot be truly severed. Not by magic. Not by will. It is not like any other bond. It can be cloaked, buried behind a wall of one's own making. But it will always remain — howling in the dark."

End of excerpt

I slam the book shut so hard that dust explodes off the spine. My hands are shaking.

Hellhound. HELLHOUND!

Draven isn't a lycan. He's not even a normal shifter. He's something older. Darker. Something the gods themselves couldn't stop. And I severed a bond that can't be severed.

Stars above.

I press a palm to my chest, but there's nothing. No spark. No echo. Just the chill spreading down my spine.

"Of course," I mutter bitterly. "Of course he's one of the

seven nightmare monsters from the pre-soul apocalypse. Why wouldn't he be?"

Neris is quiet for once. Even she doesn't have a sarcastic remark. That's how bad this is.

"I cloaked the bond," I whisper, the realization sinking in. "I didn't destroy it. I just… closed the door."

I look toward the window. Somewhere out there, the not-lycan is pacing the halls of this palace. Probably brooding. Probably shirtless. And absolutely, undeniably, still tethered to my soul.

"Great," I mumble. "I'm emotionally handcuffed to an indestructible, hellfire-born demigod with talons bigger than my face."

I rub at my temples. I'm about to have the headache of a thousand headaches.

"I need tea. And maybe a priestess."

Of course the bane of my existence picks the exact moment I'm having a meltdown to waltz into the library.

"Are you okay?" Draven asks as he slides into the seat beside me, shoving a plate of food under my nose. Steak. Dammit, that smells amazing.

Then I feel it — a touch. Light at first. Tentative. And then firmer, drawing slow, steady circles between my shoulder blades.

Relief blooms in my chest like warmth from a fire. The headache vanishes instantly.

I glance at him. He immediately pulls his hand back.

"Don't stop," I snap.

His hand returns. I melt. Just a little.

The pounding in my skull eases again. The tension in my spine unwinds. I exhale, leaning slightly into the pressure.

"I'm fine," I lie, opening the book and pushing it toward him. "You read. I'll eat. And you keep touching my back. Got it?"

He nods. Doesn't say a word. Just picks up the book like a dutiful research assistant and keeps his hand where I need it. He reads, I devour the food.

The second I swallow the last bite, he speaks.

"So the bond's not severed!"

He sounds elated. Like he just won a century old war.

I give him a flat look. "That's your takeaway?"

I gesture at the book, a second away from picking it up and throwing it at his head. "We just read that you're most probably a creature born of hellfire. That gods once lost a war to your kind. That the world could be saved or destroyed, depending on how you might feel each morning. And you're excited about the bond?"

"Everything else can be figured out," he says, voice suddenly quiet. Serious. "But I thought our bond was gone. Forever. And it's not."

His smile is small. But so full of hope. Damn him. "Of course, even if it was… it wouldn't have changed anything for me. But it's good to know it's still there." He taps two fingers against his chest.

I cross my arms and huff. He sighs and stands.

"Come on, grumpy," he says with too much charm. "Neris needs a run. I need to stretch my wings. Let's get out of here before your brain explodes."

"Fine," I mutter. "I could use a break. The High Priestess is still coming tomorrow, right?"

"Yeah. We'll show her the manuscript, let her dig through the crazy with us. Maybe she'll have something to help."

My paws barely skim the forest floor, Neris laughing in my head, wild and high.

We've been running for what feels like hours, but I'm not tired. Not even close. The trees part for me. The wind howls with me. The forest sings back to my steps. And above it all — above the forest — I feel him. A shadow of wings that circles high, gliding like a dark god against the clouds.

"I could outrun him in a race on foot," Neris pants, determined. *"He's big and fast, but I'm small and slippery."*

"You're going to crash into a tree," I warn her.

And not even a second later — bam — her side clips a low branch and she tumbles in a heap of tangled limbs and fur.

"Don't say it," she groans.

I smirk. *"I told you so."*

With a huff, I take control again and shift back. My human form returns in a ripple of heat, muscles stretching, bones cracking. I gasp through it, skin steaming in the cold air. I'm naked, of course, but I remedy that instantly when I see a big shirt hanging on the branch of a tree. They're everywhere here, ready for any shifter to use after a run.

I barely have time to shake out my hair before I hear the rush of wind.

Draven.

He lands like something out of a dream — or a nightmare, depending on the day — and the moment his boots touch the ground, he's smiling right at me.

Wings spread wide behind him. Bare chest gleaming with sweat — hmm, that dark bruise is starting to worry me.

His eyes drag over me once. Slowly. Intently. And then, without warning, strong arms scoop me off the ground.

I yelp. Loudly.

"What the hell are you doing!?" I shout as the world tilts.

He laughs and unfurls his massive wings with a thunderous snap. My stomach drops as we shoot into the sky.

"I'm giving you a new perspective, mate. See the world in a way you haven't seen it before."

The air is cold but his body is fire. Every beat of his wings sends a gust of wind past my face, sweeping through my hair, tightening the skin on my cheeks. I wrap my arms around his neck tighter. His grip never wavers.

We soar even higher.

Above the trees. Above the palace. Above everything.

The sky is endless here. Burned orange at the edges where the sun's just about to bow. And beneath us, the forest stretches like a living sea. Wild and boundless.

And gods, I laugh.

I laugh so loud it echoes into the clouds.

It bursts out of me like sunlight. Like freedom. For the first time in what feels like forever, I'm not thinking. Not planning. Not worrying. I'm just here — wind in my hair, sun on my skin, arms wrapped around the Alpha King while his wings cut through the heavens.

Even Neris is giddy, tail wagging, soaking it all in with big, bright eyes. And she's a wolf, she shouldn't be enjoying this!

In this moment, the world isn't in danger of catching fire.

In this moment, I feel light. And free.

CHAPTER 9

Draven

"Whatever she says, don't take it too seriously, alright?" I murmur to Kassira as we approach the Moon Temple nestled near the palace. "We'll figure this out. We'll find a way."

She just huffs in that infuriatingly endearing way, grabs my hand, and pulls me toward the arched entrance. "Come on, Your Majesty. Stop stalling."

The doors creak open as we step inside, and the High Priestess is already waiting — right in the center of the temple, like she's been pacing for hours.

"Welcome, my sweet darlings!" she chirps, voice far too cheery for the kind of doom-and-gloom prophecy talk we're probably about to hear. Her colorful robes shimmer like sunlight on water as she turns and glides deeper inside. "Come, come! To the Seeking Room. We'll have all the peace and privacy we need there."

She doesn't wait for an answer. Just floats ahead.

We follow in silence. Kassira's hand stays wrapped in

mine, warm and grounding, and for a moment I forget how much pressure is sitting on my shoulders. She's been doing this more and more — touching me casually, letting her fingers graze mine, smiling at me freely. Like maybe... I'm not entirely ruined in her eyes.

It's enough to keep my hope alive.

The Seeking Room is cozy, dimly lit by filtered moonlight streaming through high stained glass windows. We sink onto the soft cushions around a low table that's cluttered with sweets, berries, and delicate pastries.

The High Priestess lowers herself to the cushions with all the grace of a hundred-year-old swan and beams at us. Her gaze settles on Kassira.

"You two shine so brightly together," she says, voice dipped in awe. "You're practically bathed in light."

Kass snorts. "That's weird," she mutters, jerking her thumb toward me. "Since this big guy over here doesn't have a Mate Spark. Or so you told him."

The Priestess just smiles, unbothered. "Your shine doesn't come from the Spark," she says, tilting her head like she's listening to music only she can hear. "It's the Moon Goddess. She's blessing your bond. Offering favor to your mating."

A blessing to our mating? I forget how to breathe for a second.

"High Priestess, plea—" Kassira starts, but the priestess lifts a hand, gently cutting her off.

"Please," she says with a warm smile, "call me Camara.

The High Priestess title gets exhausting after a while, and sometimes, it's nice to just be a person again."

Kass blinks. I jump in.

"Yes, well, Camara," I say, shifting forward. "We have a situation. A serious one. And we're hoping you might have answers… or at least a direction."

Her gaze turns to me, softening with something close to sadness. "Your Mate Spark," she says, already knowing. "When I heard you'd found your true mate, I was so happy. But if the bond exists and I still couldn't sense your Spark back then… then it's not gone. It's hidden. And that kind of concealment?" She shakes her head, voice dropping. "It's not normal. It must be magic. The kind that works in shadows and leaves no trace."

Kass snorts and crosses her arms like she's two seconds from throwing something across the room. "It's not just dark magic," she says sharply. "He's a hellhound. A *hellhound*, Camara." She leans forward like she's about to drop a bomb. "And I know you know what that means. Apparently, the High Priestesses have been keeping that little bedtime story under lock and key."

Camara's eyes widen, but Kass doesn't stop.

"And to make matters worse, the magic hiding his Spark is some very old and powerful controlling magic. It shows as a red, glowing leash around the hellhound's neck. And this leash? It's covered in markings I've never seen before. And I've read everything. Every documented magical symbol, sigil, rune, curse pattern. These? Nothing matches. And it's controlling him. It blocked our bond. It manipulates his memory — he forgets me if we're apart too long." Her voice cracks. "So yeah. We need some damn help. No more secrets."

"A hellhound..." Camara whispers, eyes wide with wonder. "That knowledge... it's only passed from High Priestess to High Priestess when we take our oath. Not even the Pack Priestesses are told." Her eyes lock on me like I'm about to explode into a shift right at this moment. "How did you find out?"

"Kass found it," I say, nodding toward her. "A fragmented entry from an old journal, buried deep in the Forbidden Archives. It talked about seven hellhounds who went to war with the gods to demand souls of their own. And won."

Camara closes her eyes and exhales slowly. "Yes," she breathes. "It's true. The Moon Goddess herself gave them their Sparks. But their bonds... they were not like ours, like normal shifter bonds. Not woven from moonlight, not fragile." She opens her eyes again, face tight with reverence and unease. "They were forged in hellfire. And that's why they can't be broken. Not truly."

Her stare lingers on me for a few long seconds, like I'm the weirdest thing she's ever seen. "I can't believe I'm sitting across from a hellhound," she murmurs. "I never thought I'd ever see one."

Well, neither did I, Camara. Neither did I.

"Did you confirm it?" she asks, turning sharply to Kassira. "That he's really a hellhound? What does his other form look like?"

"Dark. Giant. Massive wings, claws like swords, scales under the fur, and stubborn as all hell," Kass says, arms crossed.

"Yeah," Camara whispers, eyes wide. "That sounds like a hellhound, alright." Her gaze shifts to me. "Draven, I assume you couldn't shift because of the magic?"

I nod once. "Right. I can summon the wings, but that's it. I can't feel him. Can't speak to him. Kass is the only one who can bring him forward. And even then, it doesn't seem to weaken the magic. We've tried."

"What happened when you shifted for the first time?" she asks, eyes narrowing.

"I severed our bond," Kass answers before I can speak, and a low growl tears out of my chest without warning. Her lips twitch like she was expecting that reaction. She shrugs. "Well, I thought I did. Turns out I just cloaked my side. He still feels his."

Camara hums, like all the puzzle pieces are clicking into place. "Yes… yes, I see it now. The bond between a hellhound and their mate, it's unlike any other. That rejection," I growl again, sharper this time, "must have cracked the leash. Not fully. But enough to let your hellhound push through. He's likely been fighting that magic your entire life, Draven. And the wings… they were the only thing he could break through with."

She pauses, thinking. "Or maybe more. Have you ever… acted against your own will? Said something you didn't mean to say? Did something without knowing why?"

My jaw tightens. I lower my head. "The day I first met Kass," I say, voice low, "I remember… this overwhelming urge to order her execution. It felt like it was the right call. But then, when I opened my mouth, I exiled her to Kunou Forest instead. It was like... like someone else was speaking for me."

"Kunou Forest..." Camara breathes.

"Yeah, that place was a real treat," Kass mutters dryly beside me.

Camara glances at her. "It may have saved your life."

I snap my eyes to her. "What do you mean?"

She turns to me. "No pure-blooded witch can enter Kunou Forest. Their magic can't reach beyond its border. It's sacred ground — forgotten now, mostly. But during the witch-shifter wars, hundreds of years ago, shifters prayed to the Moon Goddess to protect a space from all sorcery. And she answered. That forest became the only place witches couldn't touch."

She holds my gaze. "Draven... I think your hellhound forced the leash to bend. He couldn't speak. He couldn't shift. But maybe he could redirect. He got you to send your mate to the one place the witch couldn't reach."

I stare at her, throat dry.

"You may have had more of those moments than you realize," she continues gently. "Times he tried to break through. Times he tried to protect you or your mate. The leash's magic is old, powerful — but so is he." Her brows furrow, voice dipping lower.

"This isn't just rare magic. This is dangerous. And if it's built to suppress a hellhound... then someone out there knew exactly what they were doing. Oh, this is not good."

Camara starts grabbing pastries from the plates in front of her, one after another, eating like she's stressing out and sugar is her only salvation. "A hellhound being born in this era? That's already enough to shake every pack to its core," she says between bites. "But a hellhound leashed by a witch?" She swallows, eyes sharp now. "That's catastrophic. For all shifters."

Her fingers hover over another pastry, but she doesn't pick it up. "Whoever did this — they had to wait for the perfect window. And for a hellhound, that only happens once. Right after birth. When the soul is still anchoring to the body. You were vulnerable for days, Draven. Not weeks. Not months. Not years. Just days. After that, it would've been impossible."

Kass straightens beside me. "Who had access to the King's heir right when he was born?"

Camara leans back on her cushion, brows drawn together in concentration. "I remember that time," she murmurs. "Your mother insisted on keeping you secluded. She wanted time alone with you and her mate before you were presented to the public. She didn't bring you to the Moon Temple for the blessing until nearly a month after you were born."

She exhales slowly. "That means only your parents were near you. And…" Her face tightens. "A midwife. There was a woman your mother trusted. She was there for the birth. Never saw her again after that."

Her eyes snap to mine. "She must've been the one. She's the only other person who had access to you during that critical window. But I can't remember her name. She vanished afterward. You'll need to speak to your uncle. He might remember her."

A chill moves down my spine, like ice taking root. My jaw locks. "My parents," I grit out, "could their deaths have been her doing?"

Camara looks down. "It would make sense," she whispers. "Your father wasn't a fool. Given enough time, he would've seen something was wrong. Your mother, too. Especially when you met your mate — when the bond failed to activate. That witch couldn't risk it. She would've needed you alone. Vulnerable."

My hands curl into fists.

Camara continues, voice softer now. "Your uncle suspected something, you know. When you didn't shift at sixteen, he came to me. After I couldn't detect your Mate Spark, he still pushed for more answers. But nothing felt wrong. No one could feel the magic. Not even me. And your uncle... he had too much on his plate. Acting as regent, fighting off challengers in your name every other day, holding his own pack together."

I stay silent, rage simmering just under my skin.

"In the end," she finishes, "everyone just assumed you were... unlucky. The first shifter who couldn't shift. Maybe a rare case. Maybe you didn't have a Mate Spark because your other half didn't exist." She shakes her head. "We were all wrong."

And now I'm the one paying the price for it. For being leashed like some cursed dog while the woman who belongs to me... had to suffer because of it. My mate. My soul's twin.

"Wait," Kass says, brow furrowed. "Isn't your family famous for mowing through challengers like they're nothing? Why was your uncle struggling?"

"That's my father's side," I reply. "He was an only child. My uncle is my mother's brother — he was also the Alpha Prime of the Bloodwulf Pack back then. So not only did he have to run his own pack, he had to act as regent until Sierra — his daughter, Sin's sister — was old enough to take over. It nearly broke him."

I pause, the memory tugging something strange out of my chest.

I was eight when my parents died. Too young to shift. Too young to fight. My uncle stepped up without hesitation and held the throne until I was ready. And when I finally claimed it at nineteen — the youngest Alpha King in history — he threw a party for himself so loud I thought the palace would collapse from the celebration alone. I've never seen the man drunker. Or happier.

He was a nightmare during my training. Brutal. Unrelenting. Pushed me harder every day, like he was racing against an invisible clock. I used to hate it.

Now I understand it saved me.

He still serves on the Council as Bloodwulf's representative, but he only shows up for the big stuff now. High-level votes. War councils. The kind of things you can't skip.

Camara suddenly leans forward, and I stiffen as I catch her sniffing the air.

"What are you doing?" I ask, leaning back slightly.

Her face tightens. "Nothing. That's the problem. I can't sense a damn thing. No magic. No trace. My wolf can't pick up anything."

She rises to her feet. "Let's see if your Spark shows now. Shirt off."

I hesitate for a second, then do as she says. I pull my shirt over my head and stand still.

She freezes.

Her eyes are locked on my chest. On the bruise.

"That mark," she says slowly, pointing to it. "How long have you had it?"

"It showed up the day I first shifted," I say. My voice comes out low, almost hoarse. "When Kass..." I swallow. "When she cloaked her side of the bond."

"And it hasn't healed since?" she presses. "Draven, your healing is faster than anyone I've seen. This should've disappeared in seconds."

I nod once. "As you can see, it didn't."

"Could it be the leash?" Kass asks, stepping closer. Her tone is sharper now. Concern buried under irritation.

Camara frowns. "Maybe. I don't know. I've seen a lot in my life, but I've never seen this. Not even in shifters who've survived rejection."

I run a hand down my face. This just keeps getting worse.

"Let's see about that Spark now," Camara murmurs,

her voice soft with wonder as she lifts her hand and presses a single finger to the center of my forehead. "Close your eyes."

I do.

She begins to chant the old words, her finger slowly trailing down my skin. My chest rises and falls with each breath. I remember the first time she did this, when I was a teenager. I'd felt… nothing. Just cold emptiness.

But this time?

This time, the moment her palm flattens against the center of my chest — burning.

A fire erupts beneath my skin, licking at bone, white-hot and sudden. My eyes fly open and I choke on a gasp, staggering back from her touch on instinct alone.

Both women move at once.

"What happened?" they ask in unison, voices laced with alarm.

"Your hand," I manage to say, clutching my chest. "It burned. Like I was on fire."

Kass's head snaps toward Camara, fury blooming across her face. "What the hell did you do to him?"

But Camara just smiles, not startled at all. "Nothing beyond the usual ritual," she says calmly. "But this… makes sense. If your bond is forged in hellfire, then someone calling it forward would burn. That's a good sign — it means it's finally responding. It's waking up."

She pauses, but her brows knit together in a frown. "And yet… I still can't see your Spark. Not even a flicker.

It's like there's a void where it should be."

"But I feel it," I say, quietly. "The bond. I feel it now."

Camara nods slowly, like that makes perfect sense. "You should just mark each other," she says, breezy and casual.

"Absolutely not," I say immediately, my voice sharp.

Kass throws her hands in the air. "Well, I wasn't planning on it anyway, but it's nice to know you feel the same, Your Majesty," she mutters, sarcasm thick.

"Kass," I murmur, turning to her. "We don't know what this magic is doing inside me. If I mark you and it spreads? If it infects you too?" My voice breaks on the edge of that thought. "I couldn't live with that."

Her expression falters. Just for a second. I see the disappointment slip through. It guts me.

I wish we wouldn't have to deal with this. I wish we could just be normal mates, just navigating our way through the usual stuff, toward a life together.

Camara's tone softens. "It's a valid concern. But it's also possible that your mark — especially from a hellhound — could be strong enough to break the leash entirely. Your kind was very unpredictable. And powerful."

"I'm not risking my mate's life on a possibility," I snap. "Not now. Not ever."

She lifts a shoulder in a shrug. "That's your call." Then she straightens. "Now, get out."

I blink. "Excuse me?"

"I need a private word with your mate," she says, like she's shooing off a servant. "Alone."

"No," I growl.

"Yes," Kass says at the exact same time, stepping in front of me and shoving her palms against my chest. "Out."

She leans in close, eyes locked on mine, her voice dropping to a dangerous whisper. "And don't you dare use your shifter hearing to listen in. That would make me very unhappy."

Fuck, why do I love it so much when she threatens me?

I sigh and let her push me toward the door. "Fine," I mutter. "But if she does anything suspicious..."

"I'll throw her through a window," Kass replies sweetly.

She shuts the door in my face.

And I stand there, grinning like a fool.

CHAPTER 10

Kassira

I turn to the High Priestess, arms crossed, spine straight, glare sharp enough to draw blood.

"What did you see?" I ask, voice low. "What do you know?"

She smiles warmly. "You're very direct. I like that." But the smile fades as quickly as it came, her voice dropping to a hush. "That bruise... I've never seen anything like it on a shifter before. But... I could sense something from it."

My brows pinch. "What?"

She hesitates for a breath. "Draven is powerful. His body heals instantly. But that bruise... it won't. I would stake every blessing the Goddess ever gave me that if he gets hurt in that spot, the wound won't heal."

The air leaves my lungs instantly. My stomach turns to stone.

"What are you saying?" I whisper. "That if someone

stabs him there... he'd die?"

She nods once. Solemn. "Yes. I think so." She steps closer, eyes shadowed with warning. "And I don't believe it's the leash that caused it. I think it's the hellhound himself."

The ground shifts beneath me. My pulse kicks into overdrive.

"I think," she continues softly, "that you may one day be forced to choose — kill Draven... or let the world burn."

Neris growls so loud in my mind it rattles. *"I'll kill her first! She can't say that! Let the world burn to ash!"*

My hand rises to my throat, dry and tight. "No," I breathe. "No. I can't. I won't kill my mate. That's insane. What the hell are you talking about?"

Camara doesn't flinch. She meets my anger with sadness. "I don't know if it will ever come to that. But the hellhound wouldn't create such a weakness unless he believed it was possible."

She reaches out and takes my hand. Her touch is gentle, her eyes kind. "You're stronger than you think, Kassira. You could survive anything."

"I'm not strong," I whisper. "I don't even know why I was chosen to be his mate. Draven is the one who's strong. I'm..." My voice cracks. "I'm the kind of wolf a teenage pup could take down with one swipe."

Camara studies me. No pity in her gaze, only certainty. "Strength isn't always in the body. Draven has that part covered. But your strength... it's in your mind. In your instincts. That's what he needs. You balance him. That's what true mates do. They complete each other — not compete with one another."

Her words hit something tender inside of me. Six months of silence, six months of feeling like I wasn't enough... and I started to believe it. I forgot that I don't need to have unusual powers in order to be enough.

I exhale slowly. "Thank you."

"Don't thank her!" Neris snaps. *"She wants us to kill our mate, remember? We don't thank people like that, Kass!"*

My smile fades. My spine straightens again.

"I still won't kill my mate," I say, voice like steel. "Not for the world. Not for anyone."

The moment I step out of the room, I grab Draven's hand and start walking fast. No words. I don't know where I'm going, only that I need to move. Need to put space between us and what the Priestess said.

"Kass?" he asks, confused, falling into step beside me. "What did she say? What did you two talk about?"

I don't answer. I need to take him somewhere safe.

"Kassira?"

His voice sharpens. He digs his heels in. Comes to a full stop.

I tug on his hand, but he doesn't budge. Stupid mountain of muscle!

"Please," I say, barely above a whisper. "Just come with me. I need you to."

He studies me for a beat — eyes narrowing, gaze cutting straight through me. Then, with a nod, he lets me pull him again, matching my steps.

It isn't until we're standing inside the library, the door clicking shut behind us, that I realize where I've taken him.

The silence inside is thick. Heavy with words I'm not ready to say. I turn toward him and without a word, I wrap my arms around his waist and hold on like the world might end if I let go.

He freezes for a heartbeat. Then, slowly, his arms come around me. Strong. Steady. His chin rests gently on top of my head. He doesn't speak. Just waits. Quiet and patient. Exactly what I need.

I press my ear to his chest. His heart beats strong and sure beneath my cheek. Alive. Steady. As it should be. As it must remain. He can't die. Not for me. Not because of me. Not ever.

He still has groveling to do. He owes me that. He owes me a lifetime.

Neris is silent in my head, but I feel her grief coiling deep, her anxiety trembling close to tears. She's terrified. Just like me.

My voice barely rises above the hush between us. "Did you ever take her flying?"

It's absolutely not the thing I should be talking about

right now. But I can't say the other things. Not yet.

"No," he answers. Quiet. Honest. "I never took anyone else flying."

Something inside me settles at that. It shouldn't matter. But it does. That witch took so much from both of us — but she didn't take this.

I look up at him. Right into those stormy eyes. So full of questions. Of unspoken promises.

His hand lifts, thumb brushing over my cheek, gentle as a breeze. "Are you okay?" he murmurs.

No. Not even close.

I can't answer him. The words won't come.

I feel the walls closing in, I feel time running out for us.

And it hurts that he's not the bad guy I thought he was.

It hurts that he's not the monster I spent six months screaming at in my head. Not the cold, heartless villain I blamed for every sleepless night, every aching breath.

It hurts that he's actually a good man who fell victim to evil.

And I wish — gods, the dark part of me wishes he were the cruel bastard I thought him to be. Because then... losing him wouldn't hurt.

But he's not. He's clumsy. Hopeful. Quietly fierce. Loving. Paranoid as hell. And he's mine.

And I'm ready to fight for him. Neris, too.

So I rise on my toes and kiss him. Just a brush of lips. A silent plea. A selfish want. I need to feel him. Need to hold this moment, for however long it lasts.

He stills. His breath catches. But he doesn't pull away. He lets me linger. And then he's there, answering.

His arms wrap around me and pull me close. His mouth moves over mine, deeper now — the fire in his blood pouring into mine, igniting something that steals the air from my lungs.

And then — sparks.

Everywhere.

My skin burns with them, my chest snaps tight, and I gasp into his mouth as something inside me stitches itself back together.

The bond. Alive. Again.

He exhales, the sound laced with relief, and I feel the curve of his smile against my lips.

Neris sighs in my head, rolling onto her back, tongue lolling, tail wagging like she's floating on clouds.

"Welcome back," he whispers, fingers threading gently through my hair. He kisses me again. Slower. Like he has all the time in the world. Like we're not running out of it.

I pull back, just enough to breathe. "The Priestess said I might have to kill you."

He blinks. His brows draw together. "Well." He exhales. "That's one hell of a way to kill the mood, isn't it?"

A small laugh escapes me — sharp and bitter — and I drop my forehead against his chest.
"She said that bruise… it might be a weak point. That if you're struck there, you might not heal."

His arms tighten around me. "Then I won't let anything touch it," he murmurs. "I'll be careful. I promise."

But we both know careful may not be enough.

It's only two weeks later that we get the news: Alpha Parrin of the Mirenwulf Pack is dead.

"I have to go," Draven says, voice low, distant. "He was a Prime. As King, I need to be there. It's my duty."

I sit beside him in his office, cold dread pooling in my stomach. It feels like watching someone walk to their own funeral. We're not any closer to breaking the leash. We're not any closer to real answers.

"I feel like it's a trap," I whisper.

"I know," he says.

He reaches for me, pulling me gently into his lap. I don't resist. His arms wrap around me like armor, and the tightness in my chest loosens just a little.

Ever since my side of the bond flared back to life, everything between us has shifted. We're closer. Warmer. But still cautious, like two people dancing at the edge of a cliff, afraid of what might happen if they fall.

He spoke to his uncle about the midwife who attended his birth. The only outsider who had access to him in those vulnerable first days. She had dark hair, was tall, soft-spoken. Her name might've been Cerella — I'm sure that wasn't even her real name and that she wore a magical disguise. His uncle didn't know how Draven's mother met the woman or where she came from. Of course he wouldn't, there was no reason for him to know details of the midwife his sister was going to use.

I have this gnawing feeling in my gut. Like the end is near. And neither of us knows *how* it's going to end. And the cruelest part? I've started falling for him. Maybe I already had — even before the bond returned. But now I live in this agonizing limbo where I want to move further with him but I'm too afraid to do it. Not until I know the danger is gone.

Neris, on the other hand, has no such thoughts. She already decided she just wants her mate, danger or not. She wants him completely. His love, his mark, his vows, his name on our skin. Danger be damned.

I'm the one holding us back. Maybe I should just follow her instincts. Well, not the marking part. Draven made a good point with that one, I wouldn't want to find myself suddenly infected with the kind of magic that is keeping him leashed.

I tilt my head up and whisper, "Draven…"

He looks down at me, a soft smile tugging at his lips. "You said my name."

I roll my eyes. "Yeah, yeah. Throw yourself a parade

later."

I pause, my voice quieting. "I have to come with you to Mirenwulf. You can't be away from me that long — the magic will get stronger. You'll forget me again."

I lift a hand and trace his jaw with slow movements.

"We don't know what's waiting for us there. We don't know what our future is going to look like. But tonight..." I draw in a shaky breath. "I want it to be about us. No fear. No restraint. I don't want you sleeping on the floor anymore. I want to take the next step. I want to strengthen our bond."

He leans down and presses his mouth to mine. A kiss that's soft and steady, connecting our souls to each other. When he speaks again, his words are laced with warmth, curling around my heart like a promise.

"Whatever you want, my beautiful mate," he whispers. "I only live to make you happy."

He's so close I can feel the heat rolling off him, see the blue in his eyes flicker like flame. We're in my room and he's been watching me for a few minutes now. He's waiting for me to make the last move. To set the pace.

He wants me. I know he does. He's made that clear with every touch, every gentle word, every moment he waited for me to come around. Even now — even with the hunger pouring from him in waves, thick and feral and a little bit terrifying — he's still holding back. Following my lead.

I reach for his shirt and tug him closer. His lips part in a question, breath fanning across my cheek.

"Are you sure?" he whispers, voice hoarse.

"Yes," I say, honest to the bone. Because I am. There's not one doubt left in my mind about him. There's just fear for our future. But I know I want him — I am completely sure about that.

His arms wrap around me, lifting me until my feet dangle. I gasp, clutching at his shoulders. He carries me to the bed and sets me down like I'm made of spun sugar, then sinks to his knees in front of me. Massive, beautiful. And mine.

He waits, palms splayed on the edge of the mattress, watching me carefully.

I reach for him, thread my fingers into his hair, pull him up until his mouth is pressed to mine. He kisses me like he's been waiting for this his entire life. It's a little desperate, a little wild, and when his tongue sweeps over my lower lip, I can't stop a moan leaving me.

He growls, deep in his chest. It vibrates through me, making my toes curl.

He presses me back into the sheets and the world narrows to the two of us. To the heat of his body and the feel of his hands. He explores every inch — my throat, my shoulders, the curve of my waist — slow at first, then faster, greedy. I arch beneath him. I want more. All of him.

His hand slides up my thigh, pauses at the edge of my shorts.

"Tell me to stop," he rasps, "and I will. I swear it, Kass."

"Don't you dare," I whisper, sending a glare his way.

He grins, fangs peeking. "As you wish, my Luna."

He peels the shorts away, and then his mouth is on my stomach, my hips, the softest places that have never known a touch like this. I'm shaking. I want to hide, to pull away, but every time I try, he chases me, nuzzles, soothes. He doesn't rush. Not even when my nails dig into his scalp. Not even when my breath comes in high, broken gasps.

He takes his time.

When he finally moves above me, when his body covers mine and I feel the size of him, I panic a little. I freeze. The old fear returns, all the warnings I ever heard about pain and blood and how it's supposed to feel like dying before it feels like flying.

He senses it instantly. His hands cradle my face, his eyes searching mine. I force myself to meet his gaze. I don't want to run. I don't want to ruin this.

He cups the back of my neck and kisses me, softer than before.

"I'll go slow," he promises.

He does. He's so careful it almost breaks me. He moves with infinite patience, coaxing my body to open for him, letting me adjust to every new inch, every stretch, every burning, impossible moment. He whispers to me the whole time — words I don't understand, words that sound beautiful.

When it hurts, I squeeze his forearm and he stills. He holds me, his lips pressed to my temple, waiting for me. When the pain finally ebbs into something sharper, hungrier, I roll my hips into his and he groans. A sound so wrecked and hungry that it snaps the last of my fear into dust.

He fills me completely, body and soul, and I feel the bond flare to life — stitching us closer together.

I want to say something but the only thing that comes out is a whimper. He moves inside me, slow at first, then faster. Until I'm shattering around him, every part of me burning and alive. He follows the moment I cry his name in pure, pleasurable agony, his whole body trembling as he pours himself into me.

Afterward, he doesn't let go. Not even when I roll onto my back and pull him with me. Not even when my legs start to cramp and I have to kick at his shins to make him shift. He just laughs and buries his face in my neck, inhaling deep.

"Neris says you smell like fire," I murmur, running my fingers through his hair.

He lifts his head, eyes bright and wild.

"You are my fire," he says, and there's so much love in his gaze that for once, I have no snarky comeback.

This might be the first time he managed to shut me up.

CHAPTER 11

Draven

We arrive at Mirenwulf Pack in the late afternoon, the air thick with grief.

Before we left, I gave Sin a full set of instructions in case something goes wrong. He usually stays behind to manage the palace in my absence, but I brought him this time. I need someone I trust, someone who would protect Kassira with his life.

Because this trip? It reeks of a setup.

Alpha Parrin's death doesn't sit right with me. It's too sudden. Too convenient. And I know in my gut — she's here. The witch who's been playing with my life. Whoever orchestrated this has been moving the pieces for a while, and now, they're bound to make a move. I just wish we had more answers before walking into the lion's den.

We're barely in front of the packhouse entrance when the first voice cuts through the somber crowd.

"Welcome, Ven."

Amira. Of course she's the first to greet us. I feel Kass' discomfort through the bond, but she keeps her expression composed. Regal.

Amira stands beside Luna Hana, who looks like a shell of herself, pale and hollow-eyed, and beside her is the Alpha Heir — Amira's older brother, Isak. Levi lingers just behind them, noticeably separate from the group. I make a mental note of that.

I don't stop walking. I just tighten my arm around Kassira's waist and keep moving forward.

"My condolences, Luna," I say as we come to a stop before Luna Hana.

Kass's voice follows mine, soft and sincere. "I'm so sorry for your loss, Luna."

Luna Hana dips her head in acknowledgement. Her voice is barely more than a whisper when she speaks. "Thank you, Alpha. Luna. Your presence means a great deal."

"We'll hold a private dinner tonight," Hana continues. "Only family and the Alpha Primes and their mates, to honor Parrin's memory. The funeral will take place tomorrow, at noon."

I nod, but my grip on Kassira tightens.

"Amira will show you to your room," she adds.

Amira offers a small smile — too practiced to be real — and turns to lead the way.

Kass doesn't speak, but I feel the pulse of irritation through our bond. She hates this as much as I do. But what can we say? We can't very well argue with a grieving widow. So we follow.

Amira stops in front of a door and turns toward us, just as I feel that now-familiar ripple of warning roll up my spine. Instinctively, I tighten my grip on Kassira's waist, pulling her flush against me.

"I'm sorry, Ven," Amira begins, her voice too soft, too careful. "My mother hasn't been thinking clearly since it happened. I'll ask the staff to prepare a second room. For your mate," she adds, smiling — though the way her teeth grind around the word 'mate' makes it feel more like a curse.

A deep growl coils in my throat, barely contained.

The implication laced in her words nearly pushes me past the edge — that somehow I didn't accept my mate, that she doesn't have a place beside me. As if the bond is still up for debate. And the way she says my name — Ven — with the intimacy of a claim she has no right to anymore, especially after I already made everything clear to her? That is unacceptable.

"Amira," I say, voice low and laced with steel. "You've studied court etiquette long enough to know that I am to be addressed by my title. Especially in front of my mate." I let the words settle, sharp and cold. "No matter what passed between us, you will show Kassira the respect she's due. She is your Luna. She outranks you in every way. I'll let this slide once, out of respect for your grief. But there won't be a second time. And one room is enough for us."

Her smile crumbles. Her lips tremble. But I feel

nothing.

Beside me, Kass straightens. I can feel the satisfaction humming through her, even before she speaks.

"I don't care what you thought you had with my mate," Kassira says coolly. "It's over. And if you keep testing me, I'll personally see to your punishment. Funeral or no funeral."

Amira's eyes flare. "You don't have the power to order anything," she snaps. "You're not even marked. You would know that — if you'd taken the time to actually study the palace rules. Only the King can give commands."

Kass lets out a slow sigh, like she's scolding a child. Her eyes lift to mine, glinting with amusement as she blinks sweetly. "My love," she says, sugar-sweet, "if I wanted to order someone's punishment... I could, couldn't I?"

My love.

Where the hell did that come from? I like it. A lot. Too much.

I lean down, brushing a kiss to her lips. Soft. Possessive. "You can order anything you want, my beautiful mate."

She turns back to Amira with a bright, victorious smile. "Perfect. Glad we cleared that up." She flicks her hand in a casual, dismissive wave. "You can go now. We can open a door on our own."

She opens it without waiting for an answer, steps inside, and I follow — without so much as a glance back.

I don't need to see Amira's expression. I can feel it.

But more than that... Something is off. Her father just died, and yet she's playing games? Trying to push boundaries with Kass? It doesn't sit right with me.

The moment we step into the dining hall, I already want to turn around and leave. The room is full — Alpha Primes with their Lunas, Betas, heirs, and gods know who else — all dressed to impress and ready to talk my ear off. I can feel their gazes shift in our direction as we enter. Some curious, some calculating. Most of them won't be able to resist the chance to pitch a new alliance, a trade route, or some other half-baked plan.

Sin is already doing what he does best — working the room, slipping between clusters of conversation. As instructed, he's listening for anything out of place.

I take a slow, deep breath to steady myself.

Beside me, Kass chuckles, her voice low and amused. "Are the kingly duties already too much for you tonight, Your Majesty?"

I glance sideways at her and grin. "I thought I was 'your love'. No take-backs now. You made it official."

She opens her mouth to probably bite my head off, but before she can get a word out, I spot my uncle stepping in — cutting off Alpha Gradin just before he can corner us. He does it casually, but I know him too well not to catch the deliberate shift in his path.

"Nephew," he greets with a nod.

"Uncle," I reply, matching his tone. I lean in slightly. "Appreciate the rescue. Gradin would've talked until sunrise."

He smirks. "I could already see the ambush brewing. You're welcome."

Then he turns to Kassira and gives a small bow. "Luna Queen," he says, with a rare warmth in his voice. "I've heard plenty about you from my nephew. Beautiful, intelligent, kind, and strong. From where I'm standing, it seems he was right."

Kass arches a brow, smirking. "I haven't even said a word. How can you be so sure he wasn't exaggerating?"

He taps the side of his nose with a grin. "I have a nose for greatness."

Kass lets out a quiet laugh, light and genuine. And just like that, my mood shifts. Her laughter always does that to me — cuts through the noise, the pressure, the weight of everything hanging over us.

She's the calm in the storm.

Less than half an hour later, my mood nosedives.

Kass isn't seated next to me at the long table. Instead, Amira's name is printed neatly on the place card where

Kassira's should be.

Fuck this.

I pick up the card like it's something filthy and hand it to the nearest server. "Find another seat for her," I say, voice cold and clipped. "My mate sits beside me."

The server's eyes widen. He nods fast and disappears.

Kass slips into the chair beside me with a satisfied sigh and a sharp look in Amira's direction. "This woman is getting ridiculous," she mutters. "She's acting like a spoiled teenager. This is her father's funeral dinner, for the goddesses' sake."

"I know," I say, lowering my head and brushing my lips against her temple. "I'll deal with her. After the funeral."

"Can I watch?" she asks, eyes sparkling with excitement.

I chuckle under my breath. "If that's what makes you happy, you'll get a front-row seat."

"Great," she hums. "I'll bring the sweets."

Sin drops into the seat on my other side, already rolling his sleeves. "Hei," he greets lowly. "No one's acting out of pocket. At least not the Alpha Primes or their mates. My sister's still a bitch, but that's nothing new. Didn't get to corner the Mirenwulf heir yet, though. He's been avoiding too much contact."

"Keep your eyes sharp," I say. "This whole thing stinks. I don't believe for a second that Parrin's death was natural."

He nods once. "Will do."

Dinner goes about as well as a formal gathering in enemy territory can. Luna Hana offers a quiet tribute to her mate. A few Alphas speak about Parrin's leadership, his legacy. Standard posturing and mourning, all polished and proper.

But Amira? She keeps looking at me like I'm a prize she won and just misplaced temporarily.

Every time her eyes flicker to Kass, I feel a growl rising inside my chest.

This isn't just jealousy. My instincts are screaming. There's something else going on with her — something I can't ignore anymore.

She'll be going through an interrogation right after the funeral.

At least, that's the plan.

But I don't get the chance.

The last thing I remember is leaving the dining hall and walking down the hallway with Kassira, her hand warm in mine, the scent of her calming every nerve in my body as we headed back to our room.

The next thing I know, I'm swallowed in darkness.

Weightless. Disoriented.

Standing face to face with my other half.

Draxis. My hellhound.

He's furious. Drowning in wild, hot rage.

And it's not just the red, glowing leash around his neck anymore.

Now, thick glowing threads — like burning ropes — coil around his limbs, his torso, even his chest. They pulse, alive and tightening, magic seething between each layer.

I can't move, I can't say a word. I'm frozen in horror, panic slithering inside my veins.

I can only watch as my hellhound thrashes in chains I didn't even know existed. Growling. Snarling. Biting at the ropes until blood drips from his jaws.

If both my hellhound and I are here, inside my mind, who is with Kass?

CHAPTER 12

Kassira

Something's wrong with Draven.

I knew it last night, when we came back to our room. He didn't kiss me. Didn't touch me. His answers were short, clipped. Cold in a way they never were before. When I asked what was wrong, he just muttered that he was tired. Needed sleep.

So I let him.

Now, watching him get dressed for Alpha Parrin's funeral, a slow, icy dread slides down my spine, twisting tighter with every second.

I don't remember anything strange at the dinner. No one acting suspicious. Even Amira kept her distance — glaring daggers, sure, but not approaching. And yet... my instincts are screaming.

Something's wrong.

"Draven," I whisper, my fingers tapping an anxious rhythm against my thigh. "Are you alright?"

He sighs, dragging a hand down his face like he's exhausted and I'm being unreasonable. "Why do you keep asking me that, Kassira? I'm fine. Just... on edge."

When he speaks next, every word feels like a claw slicing my skin.

"How can you expect to stand by my side if you panic at every little thing?" he says, voice flat. Measured. Brutal. "You need to train. Get stronger. This isn't just about us. You're supposed to be the Luna of all shifters. And right now... I'm sorry to say it, Kassira, but you're lacking."

The words slam into me so hard I actually stagger a step back.

Pain flares inside my chest. My breath catches.

He would never — He would *never* say that.

"*Kass*," Neris whines inside my head, ears flattened. "*Look at his eyes. Please. Look closer.*"

I force myself to meet his gaze fully. And it's like falling through ice.

Cold. Distant. Unreachable. No warmth. No light. Like staring into a hollowed-out shell, wearing Draven's face.

Terror claws up my throat. I swallow it down, forcing my voice steady.

"I understand. I'm sorry."

But inside me, a storm is raging.

I don't know how or when exactly it happened, but he's gone.

The storm settles with just one thought.

I'll fight. I will tear the world apart if I have to. I'll bring him back. No matter what.

Alpha Parrin's funeral is set exactly as tradition demands.

His body is wrapped in a golden shroud, laid atop a slab of earth adorned with green leaves and wildflowers. A small clearing in the heart of the forest has been chosen — open to the sky, sacred under the eyes of the Goddess.

All of Mirenwulf stands in silence, a sea of bowed heads and heavy hearts, waiting for the final moment.

When the Pack Priestess gives the signal, every shifter present will call upon the sliver of magic inside them and channel it through the King — Draven — into Alpha Parrin's body. The shroud, the slab, his earthly remains — all of it will turn to dust and return to the soil.

From that sacred ash, something will grow. A tree. A flower. Whatever plant his soul chooses, depending on the power he carried in life.

It's one of our most sacred rites.

We are creatures of duality — both human and beast — bound together by the Spark the Moon Goddess gifted us long ago. But centuries past, the Goddess of Creation also touched our kind. She gave us a small piece of her own magic, weaving it through our blood and souls.

It's not much. A whisper of power. But it changed everything.

Before her gift, the two sides of a shifter — human and beast — waged endless war within a single body. Especially if the shifter was a strong one. Years spent fighting until one side crushed the other. Dominated. Now, we are born balanced. The magic settled the war inside us before it could even begin.

That's why our births are dedicated to the Moon Goddess, our deaths to the Goddess of Creation — and the fragile, precious thread stretched between those two moments — our lives — belongs to us alone. Ours to fight for. Ours to lose. Ours to claim.

Draven suddenly stops walking, and I stop beside him.

He looks at me — no, through me — like I'm nothing more than a shadow. When he speaks, his voice is completely detached. Distant.

"You should stand back," he says. "You don't hold an official title. It would be disrespectful to Amira, given our history, if you stood by my side. I have to stand with the family."

Something in me cracks wide open. I know it's the magic speaking. I know. But my soul doesn't understand logic. My soul only feels the rejection.

Neris whimpers and retreats, curling up in a dark corner of my mind.

I manage a nod. Mechanical. Robotic. Because if I open my mouth, I'll fall apart.

I have to stay standing. I have to find a way to bring him back. Soon. Because if I don't, I'll die from a broken heart before the witch makes him kill me himself.

He doesn't look back. Just turns and walks toward Amira.

And I'm left behind, all alone, to deal with the pain howling inside my chest.

When his arm slides around Amira's shoulders — casual, familiar — it's like being stabbed a million times over. And when he leans in and whispers something close to her ear, and I watch her face brighten, her lips lifting into a soft smile like they're sharing a secret... It feels like dying.

I'm thrown back to all those months ago when I watched them together, looking like they were the perfect couple. Like she was born to be by his side.

Did we ever look like that? Did we ever look like we belonged together?

I'm trapped in my own spiraling thoughts when Sin suddenly steps into my line of vision, blocking the sight of Draven and Amira.

His eyes — usually so full of mischief — are wrecked with emotion.

"He feels wrong," he whispers, voice raw. "Did we lose him?"

I suck in a shaky breath, but the words won't come. So I just nod. Barely, but he sees it.

Sin's lips press into a hard, thin line. His whole face

twists with something close to dread.

"Fuck," he mutters under his breath.

Then he straightens, shoulders squaring like he's preparing for battle.

"Don't worry, Kass. We'll fix this. Somehow."

He shifts closer, standing guard at my side.

And when I start trembling — when the sight of Draven still holding Amira almost breaks me all over again — Sin reaches for my hand. He squeezes gently. Just for a second.

But it's enough. Enough to drag me out of the pit. Enough to make me claw my strength back, splinter by splinter, until I can breathe again.

Because if Draven can't fight for us right now... Then I'll fight for both of us.

After the funeral ends, the crowd starts drifting back toward the packhouse, slow and heavy with grief.

I stay rooted in place, heart trapped in my throat. Waiting. Hoping. Dreading.

Draven moves toward me with measured steps. His face is carved from stone. When he motions for Amira to follow him, my knees nearly buckle.

"Be strong," Sin murmurs beside me, low enough that only I can hear.

I grit my teeth and force myself to stand still, even as I feel another piece of my soul being ripped apart.

When Draven stops in front of us, his voice is empty. Cold.

"You're dismissed, Beta."

Sin just flashes a cocky smile, like he didn't hear the command at all.

"No can do, Your Majesty. You told me to stay by the Luna's side. Even if *you*'re the one trying to chase me away." He tilts his head thoughtfully. "We really should look into that memory of yours. It's worrying, how often you forget."

Something flickers in Draven's eyes — anger, irritation, I can't tell — it's gone before I can be sure.

"Kassira isn't your Luna yet," he snaps. His gaze sweeps the people around us. He sighs, as if we're an inconvenience and he has no time for this. "Fine. Stay. I won't have to repeat myself later."

Then he turns to me. And the moment his hollow, lifeless eyes meet mine, I'm back in that ballroom. Back to the night he rejected me. Back to the pain.

"I'm bringing Amira back to the palace," he says, each word a dagger. "I hope you won't throw a fit about it. It won't go well for you if you do. It was a mistake to release her from her duties. She was invaluable to me before. And now, after her father's death, she needs something to focus on. Something to help her heal. Understood?"

Every part of me cracks. But I don't let it show. I nod, because the words won't come. They're strangled by the grief swelling inside my chest.

"Thank you, Ven. You always knew what I needed," Amira says sweetly, slipping her hand into his.

He doesn't pull away. He just turns — leading her toward the packhouse — and leaves me standing here.

Sin's growl rumbles beside me, low and menacing.

"That bitch. She's definitely involved. I'll fucking kill her."

"No," I croak, my voice barely more than air. "We can't. Not yet. Not until we find the witch and break the leash. Amira is protected by Draven right now. He would kill you before you even laid a hand on her."

Sin curses under his breath, fists clenching at his sides, as we watch Draven and Amira disappear into the crowd.

Draven left with Amira right after the funeral. He took her to the palace in his carriage. Not a word to me. Not even a glance.

If Sin hadn't stayed glued to my side through it all, I don't know if I'd still be standing.

Neris keeps swinging from rage to despair. One second she's snarling to tear someone apart, the next she's curled up sobbing in a corner of my mind. I'm not much better. The bond hurts — it's messing with our minds.

I sit frozen on the edge of the bed in my room at the palace, feet dangling just above the floor.

Sin left me here, made me lock the door behind him, gave me a secret knock to know it's him when he comes back. He said he needed to check something. See if there's anything we can still do.

We had to come back. The Royal Library is the only place that might hold the answers. I barely even scratched the surface before everything started unraveling.

But my hope is slowly seeping away. We don't have much time left.

That's where I am — drowning in those thoughts — when it hits.

A sharp, searing pain knifes through my chest, so brutal and sudden it rips the air from my lungs. It spreads like fire under my skin, wild and vicious, eating me alive from the inside out.

I know this pain. I know it too well. I lived with it for six months.

The bond — it feels betrayed again.

Tears break loose, hot and endless, pouring down my face in silent, gasping waves.

"Kass, I'm here," Neris whispers, her voice cracked and small. She wraps herself around my mind, trying to shield me from it. It's no use. Nothing can shield me from this. Nothing can protect us both.

I'm moving before I even realize it. Dragging myself through the hallways, hand scraping the walls for support, chest heaving like I'm trudging through thick smoke.

It's not enough. No breath is enough. I can't stop. I have to find him.

People stare — wide-eyed, whispering.

I don't look at them. I don't see anything except the next step forward. And the next. And the next.

The moment I shove open the door to Draven's office, I stumble to a stop, clutching my chest like it might split open.

He's kissing her.

Not just a brush of lips. Not just a mistake.

He's holding her. Tight. Like she's a treasure he's afraid to lose.

And the worst part — he knows I'm here. He heard the door. But he doesn't stop.

I watch, frozen, as if trapped inside the worst nightmare of my life. Every second that passes shreds another piece of me.

She's moving faster than I thought. I'm already too late.

"Draven," I hear myself whisper. It's broken. Raw. The sound bleeds like a deep, open wound.

Finally — *finally* — he pulls back. Presses one last casual kiss to her lips, like she's his everything, then he turns his head and looks at me.

"Kassira," he sighs, almost like he's tired. "I was hoping you wouldn't find out this way."

Amira's voice cuts the air, a cruel glint travelling through the sound. "You shouldn't barge into the king's office without permission," she says, her tone dripping with smugness. "You don't have a real rank. You need to be announced first. Then the king decides if he even wants to see you."

I don't look at her. She doesn't matter.

It's Draven I can't take my eyes off.

"What are you doing, Draven?" I whisper, barely able to hear myself over the roaring in my ears.

No flicker of doubt in his expression. No flash of warmth. Only that hollow, lifeless void that's been growing more and more since the funeral.

He straightens, and I know he's about to completely destroy me.

"I'm choosing a Queen," he says, voice so sharp it could cut diamonds. "Mate or not, Kassira, the truth is you were never strong enough to stand beside me. I was confused for a while — tricked by the bond — but seeing Amira again..."

He trails off and then smiles. *Smiles.* "...it made me realize the mistake I almost made. I can't have a Luna who's weak. Who falters. Amira was always the rightful choice. And the best part? With her... it's real. There was no bond to force me. No magic. I fell in love with her by my own choice."

Lies. The bond doesn't force love.

I want to spit the truth in his face, scream it loud enough to shatter the windows — but my throat locks up. My whole body trembles, helpless against the weight of the pain crashing down inside me.

I know it isn't really him. I know it's the magic twisting his mind, his heart.

But that doesn't stop the words from carving through me. Because it's still *his* voice. His mouth shaping them. And they burn straight through the bond and into my soul.

"You'll stay at the palace, of course," Draven says, his tone completely detached. Like I'm nothing to him. Just an inconvenience he's been forced to manage.

"It's unfortunate I'm bonded to a shifter like you," he continues, ignoring the way I'm breaking apart like glass, "but I've accepted it. I can't risk my hellhound going feral because of the bond."

"Amira agrees," he adds, almost casually. "She understands that duty comes before personal feelings. You'll be my mistress. Nothing more. You'll be there to satisfy the hellhound when needed. It's more than a shifter of your... station could have ever dreamed of."

The blade of his words twists deep, straight through my heart.

I want to scream. I want to slap him so hard he wakes up from this nightmare. I want to tear him away from her, from this madness, from the magic that's rotting him from the inside out.

But I can't.

All I can do is stand there.

Silent. Shaking.

Listening to the sound of my soul dying.

CHAPTER 13

Draven

"Draxis," I finally force out, barely holding myself together. "Draxis, stop! Stop thrashing. I need you to talk to me. Tell me what's happening."

He doesn't stop. Doesn't even spare me a glance. Just keeps snapping his jaws at the red, glowing threads coiling tighter around him, wild and desperate. Like he can't hear a damn thing.

Panic gnaws at the edges of my mind, rising faster the more threads I see slithering over him. Tangling. Binding.

I don't have time for this. I need to get out. I need to get back to Kass.

Pain lances through me, searing and endless. It burns like a shadow made of knives, carving through my flesh.

I know what it is. The bond. It feels betrayed and it's screaming in protest. The pain is constant, relentless. But every few seconds, it spikes into pure agony. Like someone's tearing my soul to pieces and then slamming it back together just to rip it apart again.

Kass... She's feeling this too. The thought guts me worse than anything ever could.

My mate. My beautiful mate is in pain because of me. Bright, brilliant Kassira. Too good for me in every way that matters. Strong where it counts. Fierce, clever, stubborn. She fights like hell even when the world stacks itself against her. She's everything I ever dreamed a mate could be. And now — because of me — she's drowning in this pain, and I can't even reach her.

How can I have all this damn power inside me... and still be powerless to save her?

A roar tears from my throat, full of fury and desperation. I charge forward and slam my fist into Draxis's snout with everything I have left.

He jolts backward with a vicious snap of his massive head, stunned for a heartbeat.

Good. We need to talk.

When he finally lifts his head, slow and dangerous, he fixes those molten silver eyes on me — and for the first time since I landed in this darkness, he sees me.

"Stupid human," he spits, drool flinging from his fangs.

I roll my eyes, the pain shredding me from the inside barely kept at bay. "Are you done now?"

He snarls low in his chest.

I start pacing in front of him, running a shaking hand through my hair. "Kass was right," I mutter. "You really are a dramatic bastard."

His growl rumbles through the air, but he doesn't twitch a muscle.

I force myself to keep moving, to breathe through the next spike of white-hot agony. "What the hell is happening?" I snap at him. "Where the fuck are we? I'm guessing inside my mind?"

"*Our* mind," he growls, voice rough, cracked with something like fury.

"Our mind," I echo grimly. "Fine. Whatever. At least you can talk normally here. That's something."

I meet his furious gaze and huff out a humorless laugh. "Nice to finally meet you, by the way. Real pleasure."

He just glares at me, muscles rippling under the mass of glowing bindings strangling him.

I square my shoulders. "Now, can you tell me about the witch," I demand. "The one who did this. To you. To *us*."

The last word sticks in my throat, because suddenly — finally — I feel it. Something thick. Tight. Burning against my skin. My hand flies to my neck. Finds it. A collar. Just like his. Burning with magic.

A fucking leash. Dragging me further from her with every breath I take. I guess it makes sense. It was probably hidden from view before. There was no use hiding it on Draxis, since he was suppressed and I couldn't shift.

"Yes, I can tell you," Draxis says, snapping weakly at the glowing binds once. "The witch bound me from speaking to others, but not to you. She would've needed a separate spell for that — and she didn't bother. Thought she was safe once our connection was cut. She thought I was locked away for good."

He lets out a rough huff, nostrils flaring. His silver eyes burn like twin stars. "The magic she used has a catch. It's powerful, it keeps us chained under her will — but it cost her. It weakened her so much that her memories bled into the spell. I saw enough of them to know the truth."

My pulse roars in my ears. Finally. Finally, a crack in this damn nightmare.

"Who is it?" I demand. "Who's the witch?"

"A bitch," he snarls. "Amira's mother."

"Luna Hana?" I ask, thrown off.

"No," Draxis growls, shaking his massive head. "Hana isn't Amira's real mother. Her true mother is a full-blooded witch. Red hair. Eyes like gold. Her name is Galla." His snout curls in disgust. "And this witch's father? He's not mortal. He's a god. One of the old ones."

A chill sweeps down my spine. "A god?"

"The God of War," Draxis spits, rolling his eyes. "He's still salty about losing that war to our kind. He knew about the two of us long before we were born. The prophecy was whispered among the gods. So he seduced a witch, made her bear a daughter, and he gave that daughter a mission."

"What mission?" I grind out.

"To steal our power. The power of a hellhound," Draxis

says, chains rattling against him as he struggles to move. "To leash us, to bind us. To take what should never have been touched and hand it over to someone under the God of War's dominion."

My stomach twists into a cold knot. "So... Galla wants our power for herself?"

Draxis scoffs, a bitter sound. "She can't. Not anymore. She burned too much of her own strength, leashing us. If she tried to take our power for herself, it would kill her instantly." He leans closer, eyes flashing. "That's why she's using her daughter."

A curse tears from my throat. "Fuck. Fuck. That bitch will kill Kassira—"

"She won't," Draxis growls, deep and dangerous. "Not yet. She can't."

He jerks against the threads around him once, frustrated. "The first time we met our mate, she could've killed her then. But now? Our bond grew, it's too strong. Killing her would rip the bond apart violently enough to break the leash. It would shatter the spell completely." His lip curls into something savage. "They won't risk it. Not before they force us to mark that false Luna. That evil bitch. Through the mark, all our power will transfer to her."

"So we could've marked Kass and transfer all our power to her?" I ask, feeling stupid all of a sudden. We could've avoided all this.

"No, the magic is weaved in such a way that our mark is safe only for Amira. It would've hurt our mate." He looks to the side, in shame. "I got too carried away once, I couldn't help myself. I almost marked her."

I clench my fists tightly, feeling the urge to punch a hole through something. Rage and helplessness burn in my veins.

"Amira knows all this, doesn't she?" I ask, my voice a low, dark threat barely disguised as a question.

"What do you think?" Draxis snaps back, all teeth and snark.

I bare my own teeth at him. "Drop the attitude, hellhound. Not the time, not the place."

I start pacing in front of him again, fury sparking in my blood. "I need answers. Everything. You said she got weak when she leashed us all those years ago. But now?" I gesture sharply at the glowing, red ropes coiled around his massive frame. "Now you're trussed up like a sacrificial boar. So how the fuck did she pull this off?"

Draxis rolls his eyes. Again. Kass was so right. Drama queen.

"Fine," he growls. "You want the short version? Otherwise we'll be dissecting this stuff until we're dust."

I cross my arms and glare at him. "Spare me the details. Short version is fine."

"The God of War — our favorite asshole — guided Galla through everything," Draxis says, voice like grinding stone. "Told her exactly when to move, who to target. Alpha Parrin was having issues with his mate. His bond with her was weak. And he had a high enough rank. Perfect victim. So Galla hit him with a love spell while he was vulnerable. Made him believe he was… having fun with his true mate. She got pregnant. Twins."

"Twins?" I echo, my gut tightening.

He nods stiffly. "One a shifter, Amira. One a witch. Her twin, hidden away. Galla dumped Amira on Alpha Parrin's doorstep like a gift basket. Somehow, Parrin convinced Luna Hana to raise her — and I'm guessing everyone in Mirenwulf agreed to pretend she was his mate's biological daughter. Probably to save the alpha's reputation."

He keeps going, voice darkening.

"Galla kept visiting Amira in secret. Training her. Preparing her."

He shifts slightly, the red ropes glowing brighter around him. "And now the other daughter — the witch — has fully awakened. Galla is siphoning her power. That's how she reinforced the spell. That's how she has enough strength to choke us out with all this crap. Unfortunately for us, that daughter of hers is very powerful."

I curse under my breath, pacing harder.

"I used to be able to break through sometimes," Draxis says, his voice lower, rougher. "I could project thoughts to you, nudge your instincts, protect us the best I could. I gave you the wings. Some of my scales. That was my biggest win against the leash before our mate cracked it and I could shift."

His silver eyes flash with rage.

"Galla couldn't act before to cut me off completely. She wasn't strong enough on her own, and her witch daughter wasn't ready yet. She had to wait. For us to lose hope. For Amira to be shoved into our lives, positioned to be our Luna. She was counting on us marking her."

He snarls, voice pure defiance now. Shining with pride.

"But she didn't plan for *her.* For our true mate. For the hurricane we bonded with. Kassira ripped their careful little plan apart before they even knew what hit them. Not even the God of War saw her coming."

A slow smile pulls at my lips. No one could ever plan for Kass.

"Galla's been preparing for this ever since we first met our mate," Draxis cuts through my thoughts. "Her witch daughter is fully awakened now — and completely under her thumb."

"She laced the Mirenwulf packhouse with magical markers. The second we crossed that threshold, we walked straight into her claws. She didn't even have to get close — she worked from the shadows."

"She killed Alpha Parrin, didn't she?" I whisper, though I already know the answer.

Draxis snorts, unimpressed. "Of course she did." He leans forward against the glowing restraints, his lips peeling back in a snarl. "She couldn't come into our territory — not without setting off every damn alarm we have. So she played it smart. Set the stage. Lured the idiot human into her trap."

I roll my eyes so hard it's a miracle they stay in my skull. "There was no getting out of it. You know that. Alpha Parrin was a Prime. If it had been anyone else, I would've made an excuse and stayed the hell away."

I drag my hands down my face, fighting the pressure

building under my skin.

"She killed our parents too," I whisper.

It's not a question. It's truth. A brutal, ugly truth that tastes like blood in my mouth. Draxis doesn't bother answering. He knows I don't need him to.

I grind my teeth, every muscle in my body locked tight. "Does she have anyone else helping her? How much of her memories did you get?"

"Enough to make me wish I could bleach my own brain," Draxis mutters. "I got almost her entire life shoved into my skull. And Sinalyn's — her other daughter —, too. That one's... bad. Just bad." His muzzle wrinkles in disgust. "But no. It's just Galla and her two daughters. No army. No secret coven."

Great. So it's just us against a psychotic witch, her brainwashed offspring, and a pissed-off god who apparently holds grudges for millennia. No big deal.

This is so fucked up. I never imagined this. I lost so much because of a stupid god's pride. I wasn't even born and this bastard already planned my entire demise and the death of the people closest to me. He made me hurt my mate. That last thought makes fury rise in me so high I can feel it cracking my bones.

I bite down on the rage clawing at my insides.

I meet Draxis' silver gaze head-on, my voice dropping into a lethal snarl.

"How do we get out of here? How do we keep Kass safe? If any of those bitches hurt her, I swear I'll burn everything to ashes. Everything. The entire fucking world can go straight to hell."

He bares his bloody fangs at me, grim and brutal.

"There's only one way to keep our mate safe."

I know what he's going to say before the words even leave his throat.

"Our death."

I grit my teeth and roll my shoulders back, no hesitation inside me.

"So be it," I say, my voice razor-sharp. "If death's the price — then death it is."

CHAPTER 14

Kassira

I don't even know how I got back to my room yesterday. I think I just ran from Draven's office. Fled.

I hate feeling like this again. Sad. Powerless. Broken.

The pain never stops — a constant, gnawing pressure that's always there inside my chest, stealing every breath.

But somehow, I managed to claw myself back enough to think through it. Because feeling sorry for myself won't save him. Letting myself drown in my own pain won't save any of us.

We need a solution. Fast.

If that bitch gets her way, Draven will mark her on the full moon — because she's not his true mate and that's the only time he could. And the full moon rises in a week. Seven days. Seven days until the end.

It took me six months last time to build up the wall around me high enough that I was able to function through the pain and pull off what I thought was a severing of the bond.

Now I have a week. And I can't even try cloaking the bond again — it would take more magic than I can scrape together, and I'm running on fumes.

I almost laugh. How I wish my side of the bond was still hidden. Cloaked so deep that none of this could touch me. But wishing's useless now.

Not only am I drowning in agony again, but now I get the bonus anxiety of knowing the clock is ticking — and if we don't stop this, the shifter apocalypse is coming.

I swear if this situation wasn't threatening to destroy all shifters, including me, I'd already be halfway to some beach, drunk off my ass and dancing terribly to some equally terrible music.

Dammit, who am I kidding? I couldn't leave Draven behind. Not after getting to know him. Not after seeing the real him. That stubborn, silly, maddening man. He showed me a glimpse of a possible future between us so bright that I'd regret it forever if I didn't fight for it.

He didn't ask for any of this. Neither did I.

But of course this had to happen to me.

Ever since Dad died in that stupid accident, and Mom wasted away from the grief of losing her mate, my life's been one long, slow fall downhill.

I was left with a bakery job I never wanted but had to keep — because, well, a girl's gotta eat.

Instead of furthering my studies and going into research, I had to pull up my big girl pants and be an adult.

And then my mate didn't show. And when he finally did... He turned out to be a cursed hellhound king.

Why couldn't I have just gotten a normal mate? One who forgot our anniversary, killed a rabbit to apologize, and got smacked upside the head before I kissed him and forgave him?

The anger flares up, cutting through the pain. I grab the book I was trying to read and hurl it at the wall so hard that the spine snaps and pages fly everywhere.

I will find a way out of this and when I do, I'll sic Draxis on that red-headed bitch and watch as he digs his claws into her and drinks her blood.

"What if we force Draxis out?" Neris pipes up suddenly, her voice strained with pain.

I pause, considering.

"Risk Sin's life again?" I murmur, then shrug. "He'd probably be fine with it. But with how much stronger the magic is around Draven now... would it even work?"

"We'd need an exit plan," Neris gasps through another bolt of pain. *"In case it doesn't."*

Before I can answer, there's a knock at the door — three short in quick succession, two with long pauses. The knock Sin told me to memorize. The only one I'm supposed to trust.

It's cute that he thinks a locked door could stop a cursed hellhound. Men really are idiots sometimes.

I open the door, and there he is — arms loaded with books.

He marches straight to my bed and dumps them there without ceremony. Pages crinkle under the weight.

"This is everything I could find on old magic," he says, jerking his thumb toward the mountain of forbidden knowledge. "Scraped it from the restricted section when no one was looking."

He scans the disaster zone that is my room — every surface buried under open books and frantic notes.

"Any luck with the others?" he asks, already picking up a thick, dusty tome.

"That would've been too easy," I mutter, closing the door.

"Well, fuck," he says, dragging a hand through his hair. "Alright, come on. Two pairs of eyes are better than one." He plops down on the edge of the bed, flipping a book open.

"Sin." I say his name softly, and he looks up immediately, alert.

"We don't have time anymore. I think—" I swallow hard. "Neris and I think we should try to force Draxis out. Like before. During the training."

His eyes go wide. His whole body stiffens.

"Fuck, Kass." He exhales sharply, raking his hand down his face. "He's so much worse now. We have no idea if it'll work. And if it doesn't…" He shakes his head. "He'll have an official excuse to kill me. And then you'll be alone."

He says it like it's just a fact. No fear.

He shrugs one shoulder, almost casual. "Don't get me wrong — I really, really don't want to die." A grim smile curves his mouth. "But more than that, I don't want you left to deal with this alone."

He tosses the book he's holding back onto the bed, gets up and steps closer, standing right in front of me.

"I mean it, Kassira." His voice drops lower, rough with emotion. "You're our best shot. Maybe our only shot. But you'll need help. And it's not just about saving Draven — though Goddess knows I love that bastard — it's about saving all of shifter kind."

Well, that certainly takes the pressure off.

He clenches his jaw for a moment. "And I really don't want all of us to end up like zombies bowing to some evil witch."

"Then I could just mark him by surprise," I snap, throwing my hands in the air. I swear I'm about to start setting things on fire.

Sin grimaces. "That's a last resort. I mean, final-final. Hail-Moon-Goddess-level desperate. He was right about one thing — if you mark him, the magic could infect you too."

He drags in a breath, his frustration crackling between us.

"We still have a week. If we don't have another way by then, fine. Mark him."

I shake my head, my voice coming out low and raw. "I can't wait a week, Sin."

It's the truth that's been chewing through me all night. "I can barely concentrate long enough to read a page. Between the pain... and the rage at that bitch and her games..." I clench my fists at my sides. "I need him back. Even if it's just so I can kick his royal ass across the palace courtyard. Then maybe..." My voice catches. "Maybe I'll figure out if there's anything left of us."

My eyes lock onto a tiny freckle on Sin's forehead, and I glare at it like it's responsible for my entire life falling apart.

"And if I can't get him back," I mutter darkly, "then I'll find a way to make that whore bleed and turn her into mulch before I die."

A small, crooked smile tugs at Sin's mouth — the kind that says he's both worried about me and weirdly proud.

"You're a bloodthirsty little thing," he says, almost fondly. "Just like that spunky wolf of yours."

He glances over my shoulder for a second before meeting my eyes again, fierce and steady.

"Fine," he says. "Let's try it. Let's force Draxis out."

Relief and dread slam into me at once.

"Grab a few books you think might help," he adds. "If this goes sideways — and it will, I'm sure of it — I've got a way to get us out fast. Because we won't be able to stay here after."

I smirk and smack his chest lightly with the back of my hand.

"Good boy, Sin."

He growls under his breath, glowering at me like I just insulted his ancestors.

"Don't play around like that," he snarls. "My wolf is vicious."

"Sure," I say sweetly, grabbing a stack of books. "Vicious like a big, angry puppy, I'm sure."

He curses under his breath, but he's already moving. "You haven't even met him," he grumbles.

We find Draven walking down a wide hallway, Amira glued to his side. She's talking a mile a minute, smiling like a damn hyena, but he's clearly not listening. He moves like a marionette with broken strings — jerky, hollow-eyed, completely wrong. Anyone with half a brain could see it now. Even the other shifters passing by shoot him sideways glances, whispering to each other.

The subtlety from before is gone. Now the rot is obvious.

I don't waste time. I grab Sin by the wrist and drag him in front of them.

"Hello, Draven," I whisper, smiling sweetly at the man who's supposed to be mine.

His eyes don't even flicker.

There's no use for other words. I turn sharply — and

kiss Sin.

Deep. Messy. Tongue and moans and desperate fingers clutching at each other like we're about to tear our clothes off in the middle of this hallway. Sin doesn't miss a beat. His hand tangles in my hair, pulling just enough to make my knees threaten to give out. His teeth scrape over my lower lip, and the sound that rips out of me is so obscene, so raw, that if anyone still doubted our act, they're now scandalized for life.

"Oh wow. This is disgusting," Amira spits somewhere in the background.

She can go choke on her own venom for all I care.

And then — low and rumbling, almost buried under the noise — I hear it. A snarl.

I crack one eye open and steal a peek.

No Draxis yet. Just Draven, standing there, fists clenched so tight his knuckles turn white, his breathing ragged. The empty look is flickering — like a lightbulb about to die.

Close. But not close enough.

"Grab my breast. Take it up a notch," I whisper against Sin's mouth.

Sin freezes for a heartbeat — just a breath — then, to his everlasting credit, he does it. Full-on handful, squeeze and everything. I moan shamelessly, grinding against him like I've never heard of public decency.

I deserve an award for this performance. A shiny one. Preferably handed to me by a very repentant Draven after we're done saving his royal ass.

"Ven, what—" Amira's screech cuts off with a blood-curdling snarl tearing from Draven's throat.

Bingo.

I pull away from Sin and whisper, "Stand behind me."

"Remember what I said, Kassira," Sin growls low, eyes flicking to Draven, tense and ready.

"Yeah, yeah. If things go south, I grab your hand," I mutter, waving him off.

My heart shatters when I look at Draven.

He's trying to shift.

Trying.

His fangs snap forward and retreat again and again. One massive wing bursts from his back, but the other hangs limp, mangled. His claws come halfway out before sliding back into trembling fingers. Blood pours from where he rakes at his own chest, thick rivers dripping onto the floor.

He growls. He howls. The hallway shakes.

And still... Draxis can't break through.

Tears blur my vision. My fists clench tight at my sides.

Please, Draxis. Please.

"*He can't,*" Neris whispers inside my head, her voice crushed by helplessness. "*He can't break through the leash this time.*"

The scream Amira launches at me slices through my

grief.

"You just couldn't help yourself, could you?!" she shrieks.

I whip my head toward her, baring my teeth.

"Shut the fuck up, you stuck-up bitch!" I snarl back. It's the first time I've even acknowledged her since the funeral.

Her eyes gleam with pure hatred.

"I knew it. I should've had him bury you in the darkest hole under this palace," she hisses. "Your days are numbered, runt."

And then she shifts — fast, snapping into her wolf form — and lunges straight for me.

Before she can reach me, Draven moves.

He grabs the back of her wolf neck and hurls her through the air so violently the wall she slams into cracks all the way up to the ceiling.

Oh, I like that.

She slumps to the ground, unconscious, nothing but a heap of fur.

Who's the runt now, you stupid shrew?

My heart pounds so hard it feels like it might grow legs any minute now and burst out of my chest.

I snap my eyes back to Draven — focused back on the mission — and take a step forward.

"Draven," I whisper, pouring every ounce of pain, hope, and desperation I have into his name.

Sin grabs my arm before I can reach him.

"Not yet," he growls. "Too dangerous."

I shake him off, stubborn fire rising inside me.

"I'm going," I say, voice hard as iron.

But before I can take another step, Draven's head jerks back — so violently that the crack of his neck snapping echoes down the hall. His entire body freezes. No more growling. No more trying to shift. No more fight.

And then it appears — that cursed leash materializes around his neck like it's been called from the depths of hell, burning bright against his skin.

A voice slithers through the air. Cold. Mocking.

"Well, this is unfortunate."

I jerk toward the sound and watch in horror as a red-headed woman, just like Amira, steps out of the shadows behind Draven. Or... no. She doesn't step — she pieces herself together, like she's sewing her own body out of darkness.

My stomach turns. My knees threaten to give out.

When she fully forms, my horror deepens.

She's holding a glowing red thread — and it's connected to Draven's leash. When she tugs it, his entire body jolts like a puppet on strings.

She does it again, smiling wickedly, her dark eyes glittering with malice. She's not just controlling him. She's showing me that he's hers now.

A strangled growl rips from Draven's chest — low,

broken. He's fighting it. Fighting her. But the leash tightens again and cuts him off.

"Ah, ah, ah," she tuts, tugging once more like she's disciplining a pet. "Be a good little hellhound. Listen to your master."

She turns to me, smiling with the kind of sweetness that could cut through bone.

"You're such a troublesome little wolf," she purrs. "When he first met you, I didn't bother paying attention. You were too weak to matter."

The sweetness vanishes, her face twisting into something dark and vicious.

"But it turns out you're stubborn, aren't you? Stubborn enough to be a thorn in my side."

She steps closer. I can feel the weight of her power pressing down on me.

"Don't worry," she says, voice suddenly bright again, like she's sharing delightful news. "You'll only live a few more days. And when the time comes..." She grins, teeth flashing like knives.

"I'll get to watch the hellhound rip you apart."

Before I can react, she tugs hard on the leash.

"Go, hellhound. Get her for me." Her voice drops into a sharp command. "And kill the Beta."

My heart seizes in my chest.

Draven lunges. Claws bared. Murder in his eyes.

I can't even scream — the sound gets trapped deep

inside me.

But he stops suddenly. Inches away from me.

Frozen, hand poised to strike — his muscles twitching slightly, like something is holding him back.

Between us, a faint shimmer flickers into existence. A thin, almost invisible shield, woven from strands of blue light.

Magic. Not the witch's.

Sin grabs my shoulder and squeezes hard.

"We have to go, Kass. Now," he says, low and urgent.

His other hand is stretched in front of him, feeding more of his magic into the shield separating us from Draven.

"*His eyes, Kass,*" Neris whispers inside me. "*Look.*"

I look — and almost collapse. She's right. Draven's eyes aren't hollow anymore. They're haunted. Bleeding agony, screaming pain. So much pain I feel it like claws dragging across my heart.

Without thinking, I reach out. I just want to touch him. Even if it's for the last time.

"Don't." His voice — raw, broken — cuts straight through me.

My hand freezes midair. Tears pour down my cheeks, hot and helpless.

"You have to kill me, Kass," he rasps, every word a wound. "Now. It's the only way. Please. I need you safe. I tried. I can't break through. Not enough. Draxis knew.

The mark on my chest—" His voice splinters into a desperate, tortured sound. "Please, Kass."

"No," my voice sounds stronger than I feel. "You're mine. You're not hers. You don't belong to her. You don't belong to anyone but me. You and Draxis — you're mine."

He flinches like my words physically hit him.

He turns to Sin, eyes pleading. "Sin, you do—"

Before he can finish, his head jerks back and a choked, feral noise escapes him. The leash tightens mercilessly.

"Sinalyn!" The witch's voice lashes out.

From the far end of the hall, a young woman steps into view. Dark hair limp around her face. Shoulders bowed. Moving like each step hurts.

She passes Amira's still unconscious wolf form without a glance. Stops beside the witch. Offers her arm, silent and resigned.

The witch grabs her like a vulture ripping into a corpse, nails digging so deep that blood beads instantly.

The girl — Sinalyn — lifts her head.

Our eyes meet. There's pity in hers. Real pity. She mouths two words: *I'm sorry.*

And then the witch starts chanting. Soft red light coils around Sinalyn like a noose. A glowing sigil burns into her forehead.

My heart skids and crashes into my ribs.

"She's channeling her," I breathe. "She's boosting herself—"

I whip toward Sin. "We need to go. Now!"

But he's not moving. Not even blinking.

He's staring at Sinalyn like she's the only thing he can see.

"Sin?" I shake his arm hard. "Sin, come on—"

He doesn't even flinch.

Behind us, a deep, guttural growl rips through the hallway — and the air itself seems to thicken with dread.

I turn just in time to see Draven.

His eyes. Gone completely red. No white left. No silver. No storm. Just pure, blood-hungry rage.

He's clawing at the shield now. And judging by the cracks spidering through it, he'll break through in seconds.

"Sin, snap the fuck out of it!" I scream, yanking at him with everything I've got.

"*We're dead,*" Neris deadpans.

"She's my mate," Sin whispers.

I blink at him, stunned.

Oh, for the love of the goddesses. Seriously? This? Now?

Leave it to the universe to find a way to kick me in the teeth while I'm already face-down in the mud. To make everything a million times harder. And messier.

"Sin," I grit out, dragging his face toward mine, "your brand-new love story will have to wait because we're about to become hellhound chew toys."

He blinks once, twice — and then the shield between us and Draven shatters with a deafening crack.

A low growl rips from Sin's chest, growing louder, deeper — until it bursts into a full roar. Before I can even blink, he shifts.

One second, he's a man. The next, a massive white wolf, his clothes shredded to dust around him.

He lunges straight for the witch. And all I can do is stand there, useless, horror ripping through me.

The witch jerks on Draven's leash.

Draven whirls — and attacks Sin.

Oh, Goddess. He's going to die. Sin's going to die, and then I'll die, and then it'll just be the witch and her pet hellhound, turning the world to ash.

I suck in a gasp when Sin dodges at the last possible second, slipping under Draven's claws like a shadow.

Not only that — he actually sinks his teeth into Draven's shoulder, drawing a brutal spray of blood.

Draven releases a snarl that shakes the floor and swings back with deadly claws — missing Sin's throat by a breath.

And then — I blink. Blink again.

What the *hell* am I looking at?

Sin shifts again. Not back into a man. But into a white fucking dragon.

A dragon. In the middle of the palace. Oh, stars.

His wings snap open, blowing a massive hole in the ceiling, sending glass and debris flying like shrapnel. The windows explode outward. Screams echo down the hall.

It's chaos. Horrifying chaos. Mayhem.

Neris, bless her smart furry ass, drags us back just in time to avoid being shredded into confetti by flying stone and steel.

I stand there like an idiot, hand clamped over my mouth, heart hammering in my ears.

I brace myself and prepare to shift and… I don't know? Join the fight? Run?

"We'll be crushed in seconds," Neris says, voice detached. *"It's been good knowing you, Kass. Life with you was anything but boring."*

I jump nervously from one foot to another, trying to decide what the hell to do. I'm not built for battle. My weapon is my mind. And that's when I'm not panicking and I can use it properly.

Sin shifts again — back into a wolf — without missing a beat. Back and forth, dragon to wolf to dragon again, faster than anything I've ever seen.

"What the hell is he?!" I whisper, wild-eyed.

Sin and Draven tear into each other — claws, fangs, fury. There's blood everywhere, slick and glistening. Neither giving an inch.

The witch finally shrieks — a sound like nails digging into my skull — and rips open some swirling black hole beside her. She grabs the girl, Sinalyn, and throws her into it like she's nothing more than trash.

Sin howls, lunging to follow, but Draven tackles him mid-air, dragging him down hard.

I scream when I see it — Sin's claws sink deep into Draven's chest, dangerously close to the blackened mark. My breath catches.

The witch snarls and flicks her fingers. Sin is blasted across the hallway, slamming into the stone with a sickening crack.

He's up again instantly, blood dripping down his side — snarling, feral.

And I run. I run like the flames of hell are licking at my heels.

"Sin!" I scream, stumbling over rubble. "Sin, we have to leave! Now!"

For a heartbeat, he doesn't seem to hear me. His wolf is out for blood, blinded by fury and heartbreak.

Then — he stutters. His head snaps toward me.

He heard me. Thank the Goddess.

I reach him, grabbing his arm, breathless.

"Sin, we'll come back for her," I gasp out. "For both of them. But if we die here, we won't save anyone. Please."

His jaw tightens. His whole body vibrates with rage.

I shove the vial of blood into his hand — the one he gave me earlier, just in case.

It's Draven's blood. He's the one who came up with this plan, long before everything went to hell. A last resort if things ever got too bad. If I ever needed to disappear.

Sin's grip tightens around the vial, his jaw clenching hard enough I hear it crack.

He can wield blood magic. Something no shifter should ever be able to use. I've never heard of it. And yet somehow, Sin can. Draven's blood — pure hellhound, powerful — gives him enough strength to teleport us anywhere in less than a heartbeat.

I glance at the witch. She's already yanking hard on Draven's leash, making him stumble, his body jerking like it's broken.

"Please, Sin," I whisper, popping the cork and pouring a few drops of blood into his open palm. "Let's go."

He looks wrecked. Fury and grief tearing through him in equal measure. But the second the blood touches his skin, his magic stirs — wrapping around us like a storm.

The blood rises, splitting into a thousand tiny droplets. They shimmer in the air around us, spinning faster and faster, a cyclone of shadows.

Sin grabs my hand. I squeeze it hard through my panic.

The hallway vanishes and a second later, we're crashing into the cold, damp earth of Kunou Forest.

I drop to my knees. Then to my back. Panting. Shaking. Trying to pull air into my dying lungs.

"We have to kill him," I gasp, staring up at the endless tangle of trees above me. "Kill him — but also keep him alive."

Sin staggers a few feet away, hand braced against a

tree, his chest heaving.

"That's how we break that leash," I whisper, the words tasting like ash. "That's how we win."

CHAPTER 15

Draven

I'm so tired. Every muscle feels like it's been shredded and stitched back together with acid. Even keeping my head up feels like too much.

I don't know where I am. I don't know... anything.

My eyes drift to the beast in front of me. He's massive — nearly swallowed by thick, glowing red threads that pulse like veins made of fire.

His head hangs forward, limp. Eyes closed. Like every breath of life inside him was smothered a long time ago.

I glance down.

Same red threads. Coiled tight around my chest. My arms. My throat. I'm stuck in place, I can't even twitch a finger.

Panic flares, but it dies before it can reach my limbs. I'm too far gone for that. Too empty.

Why am I here?

Who... am I?

Kassira

I'm furious. Heart-shattered, soul-bruised, and every inch of me aching. But mostly — I'm pissed.

I storm through Kunou Forest, branches snapping beneath my feet, rage pulsing through every step.

Sin follows in silence, not a word escaping him.

My thoughts spin in violent circles, darkening the edges of my vision. Draven asked me to kill him. He looked me straight in the eyes and begged for death. My mate begged me to kill him. My soulmate. It broke my heart. Shattered it in pieces so small that even grains of sand are giant in comparison.

But in that wreckage, an idea sparked. Dangerous. And also absolutely desperate.

Magic can't follow someone into death. It doesn't belong to that realm — it belongs to the living. Thanatos, the God of the Underworld, doesn't tolerate magic slipping through his gates. He doesn't like it. It's too unpredictable.

There were witches once who tried to cheat him — binding magic to their souls and crossing over. He burned them to ash. No soul. No afterlife. No rebirth. Just smoke and screams left behind. And those screams lingered for months, echoing from the gates of his realm like a twisted warning.

Curses are also snapped clean the moment death touches the soul. And that's the loophole I'm clinging to. That's what might free Draven.

Except death is unpredictable. Thanatos is greedy. And Draven... Draven is powerful. The kind of soul Thanatos would love to keep.

All these thoughts feel like they're digging holes inside my skull. A sharp scream rips out of me, splitting through the quiet trees. I grip my hair, pulling so hard it stings.

"How?" I cry out, breath ragged. "How do I kill him and bring him back?"

I spin to face Sin, eyes burning, desperation bleeding from every inch of me. "Tell me. Tell me how, Sin. Please."

He's buck naked and painted in blood. His wounds already closed up — alarmingly fast — but the blood stayed. At least until we get to my small den near the river. The place where I spent six months getting ready to completely leave Draven behind. And now, in that same place, I'll get ready to bring him back. Somehow. I'm counting on that big brain of mine that everybody's been talking about to think of something.

Sin's eyes are too sad. Too heavy. I don't like seeing him like this.

"Wasn't there a guy... centuries ago?" he murmurs. "He brought his human mate back to life? I swear I heard that story somewhere."

"That's a bedtime lie," Neris scoffs from inside my head. *"A myth for cubs who cry too much."*

My shoulders sag. "Yeah," I sigh. "There's a tale that gets passed around. But even if it had a grain of truth, that guy was a fallen god. Kind of helps when Thanatos is your brother and picks up your calls."

The bitterness in my voice tastes like poison.

For a second, I think about collapsing right here — just dropping into the dirt and howling at the sky until the Moon Goddess gets so fed up with me that she fixes everything just to shut me up.

But I don't have time for drama. Not now. Not when the full moon is just days away.

I suck in a sharp breath, straighten my spine, and keep walking. The weight of the impossible presses against my shoulders, but I push forward anyway.

Because if no one's ever done it before, then I swear I'll be the first.

I stop at the entrance to the den I once called home. Funny how it feels even smaller now. I didn't think that would be possible.

"Excuse the mess," I mumble toward Sin and walk in like I never left.

It's not much. Just a shallow hollow in a big rock, cluttered with donated scraps — blankets, a few rusted pots, cracked pans. Things kind-hearted shifters leave at the edge of the forest for the exiled. You learn to survive with what you're given.

And the perk of being a shifter? You don't need a bed when your wolf doesn't care about thread count.

Sin grabs a blanket, wraps it around his waist, and leans on the wall with a sigh that's way too heavy.

"It'll be okay, Sin," I tell him, though I sound like a liar. "We'll find a way."

His silence is louder than anything I could say.

"Every two months," he whispers, voice hoarse.

I frown. "What?"

He looks at me, and the grief in his eyes makes my chest ache. "Every two months, I went to the Pack Priestess. The High Priestess, too. Just to check. Just to make sure my Mate Spark was still bright. That she was still out there, waiting for me like I was waiting for her. I even traveled to the edge of the realm searching for her. Several times."

His jaw tightens. "And now she's here. Working for the bitch trying to kill us all."

"We don't know that," I say gently. "Not for sure."

"She stood there, Kass. She let herself be used. She knew what she was doing." He growls low, something feral twitching in his eyes. "I can't believe I'm mated to a fucking witch."

"Hey!" I snap. "It's not her fault she was born that way. Not all witches are evil, you know that. Stop being a prick. Maybe she needs help."

"She mouthed to me that she was sorry," I whisper. "Right before the witch strengthened her hold on Draven."

He doesn't answer. He just mutters, "Doesn't matter. Not now. Draven's what we focus on. The witch now has access to his Alpha Command. She can control every shifter — except me. And you, of course. No one can command their own mate."

I widen my eyes.

He pauses.

"Why wouldn't the Alpha Command work on you," I ask. "Draven is the King. The Alpha of Alphas. It works on all shifters. All of them."

"It just doesn't," he says too fast. Too flat.

I narrow my eyes. "You're withholding information. Important information." I throw my hands up, pacing a tight line across the dirt floor. "What the hell are you, Sin? How come you have two beast sides? That's never been heard of. And don't even get me started on the blood magic — that's witch territory. Dark witch territory."

He doesn't even flinch. Just crosses his arms, his expression unreadable. "What I am isn't what matters right now."

"That's crazy talk," I spit. "If your powers can give us an edge, then it matters. Don't pull the noble mystery act on me. You've seen what we're up against."

"And you've already seen what I can do," he counters, voice calm but hard. "That's what we use. That's what matters."

I glare at him for a few more seconds, then throw myself down onto one of the threadbare blankets, exhaling hard through my nose.

"Fine. I won't pry into your secrets if you don't want to share with the class, Sin. But damn!"

I pause. Something hits me. My eyes slide toward him.

"Wait..."

He looks at me, wary.

"Can your dragon breathe fire?"

His silence stretches just a little too long.

"Oh my Goddess," I breathe, leaning toward him.

A slow, wicked smile spreads across his lips. It sends a shiver down my spine.

"My dragon breathes Shadow Fire, Kass," he says.

My jaw hits the floor. I blink at him. Twice. I'm dangerously close to squeaking in terror. Neris covers her eyes with her paws and groans.

"The black flame," I whisper.

He nods once. "Yeah."

Oh, stars above. This guy is just a treasure of terrifying things. Shadow Fire is the stuff of nightmares. It's feared in all the known kingdoms. Probably the unknown ones, too. It doesn't just burn — it rots the flesh until it slides off the bone. And then it rots the bone. And then the soul. It's the kind of agony that makes even demons shiver.

I swallow hard. "Thank you for not using it on Draven," I mumble, my voice about two octaves too high.

He smirks. "I barely held it back. My dragon was losing his mind during the fight." Then his smile drops. His eyes darken.

"He wanted to get to our mate," he says, voice lethal.

He turns to glance out into the forest, then back at me. "I'm going to wash off this blood. You start working that big brain of yours. We need a plan, fast. The witch can't come into Kunou Forest, but now she's got control of Draven's Alpha Command. She can send a whole army of shifters after us and they'll follow her orders like puppets."

He starts walking away, then adds, almost casually, "I'll keep a shield up around the den. Should be enough to hide us for the measly seven days we have left before everything truly goes to shit."

And just like that, he disappears into the trees.

"He's just a delight, isn't he?" Neris deadpans.

"He's upset about his mate," I mutter. "Try to be compassionate."

"I would," she says, *"if the end of the world wasn't hanging over our heads. And while we were busy surviving that entire madness? We forgot the books. The ones we stashed away, to take with us when we had to flee to save our asses."*

I groan and drag both hands down my face, exhaustion crashing into me.

"Great. Fantastic. We'll just have to dig through our own heads then. And hope something in there tells us how to kill someone and then bring them back — preferably without turning them into a soulless husk."

Neris grunts. *"Easy stuff."*

Five days later, we have nothing. Zilch. Nada. Not a plan, not even a whisper of one.

"We truly are doomed," I wail, banging my head against the cold wall of the cave-den. Repeatedly. "Just leave me here to fossilize."

Well, Draven and Draxis are doomed. Sin is prepared to shoot Shadow Fire straight at them in order to finish this. Says it's what Draven would want. I get it. I do. But I still feel like crying.

"I'm sorry, K—"

Sin doesn't finish. Because something black and smoky starts curling into the air between us. Magic.

We're both on our feet in an instant.

"What the hell is that? How is magic forming in this place," I hiss, backing up.

The smoke pulses and twists until a translucent figure starts to flicker through it. In and out, like a broken candle flame. It's a woman. *Her*. Sin's mate.

She finally stabilizes, turned toward him. But then she turns to me. And stays focused on me.

"Okay, no. What is this?" I demand, voice sharp. "How are you doing this?"

"Hello," she says gently, voice soft like a feather. "I'm sorry for the intrusion. I'm astral projecting."

She tucks a strand of dark hair behind her ear. "My mate bond," she stops and peeks over her shoulder at Sin, before correcting herself, "*our* mate bond gave me just enough leeway to be able to project myself here. You're hidden well. It took a lot of time and energy to find you. Even with the bond guiding me."

Sin's voice drops to lethal levels. "What do you want?"

She doesn't look back at him. Her eyes stay on me.

"You have to kill your mate," she whispers. "If you don't, we all die. She'll take the power of the hellhound and with it, she'll be able to create hellfire. She won't stop with the shifters — she'll make the entire world fall for the glory of her father, the God of War."

She glances over her shoulder like someone's watching. "If—"

"Nope." I cut her off with a snarl. "You don't get to demand that of me."

I take a step forward, fury vibrating in my bones. "I don't want to kill my own mate." A surge of frustrated defiance rises inside me. To hell with this whole situation. "Fuck the world. If my mate dies, then you can die, too. Everyone can fucking die!"

I raise my chin and scowl at her. My voice is shaking. My hands aren't. "I will not kill Draven. Not if I can't bring him back. Take your plan and shove it up your astral behind!"

She blinks. Once. Then twice.

Another strand of hair gets tucked nervously behind her ear. "You didn't let me finish," she says, her voice quiet, almost pleading.

Sin steps toward me, and Sinalyn flinches when he enters her line of sight.

Guilt tugs at me — I might've snapped too harshly. But being this close to losing Draven, and still not having a way to save him, is turning my brain into a battleground. I'm running out of sanity.

"Then finish what you came to say and get out," Sin snarls, venom dripping from every word. He stops at my side, arms crossed tight across his chest like he's holding back the urge to rip her apart.

Sinalyn drops her gaze. When she speaks, she brings her eyes back up to me, still not looking at him.

"I didn't think you'd be willing to kill your mate," she says quietly. "Not if he stayed dead. But you're the only chance we have to win against my mother." She takes a shaky breath. "There was no hope before. But the hellhound created a weak spot — his chest. I saw it in the fight."

Oh, stars! The witch is her mother?! This just keeps getting worse.

"Shadow Fire could finish the job just as well," Sin snaps, voice cold enough to freeze the cave.

Sinalyn flinches again and casts a quick glance his way before dropping her gaze. "Even if you had it, Shadow Fire wouldn't rot a hellhound," she murmurs. "And my mother... she's shielded. Layers of protection are woven around her and my sister. You'd never get close enough. She needs to be weakened. If the king dies, even for a moment, the magic tethered to him will break and recoil. It'll lash back at her. That's when she'll be most vulnerable."

Her hands twist together, knuckles white. She looks around like someone's watching, then locks eyes with me and speaks faster, urgent.

"You're the only one who can get close enough. He's very deep under the spell now, but he'll still hesitate to hurt his mate. You'll have seconds, maybe less. You need to kill him *and* mark him at the *exact same time*. Not before — the magic will infect you, too. Only my sister is protected from it. And not after — it would be too late. He would remain dead. But if you do it at the same time as killing him, the bond will anchor him to you. It'll be complete on your side and it'll drag him back."

Her head tilts sharply, like she just heard something. Her whole body stiffens.

"My time's up," she whispers, already flickering.

"Wait — why are you helping us?" I ask, my voice

sharper than I intend.

She looks at me one last time, something raw and aching in her eyes.

"Because I want to be free." And she vanishes — just like that. Swallowed by smoke.

We stand there in stunned silence, staring at the space she left behind, until Sin finally speaks.

"She's lying," he mutters. "She has to be. This is some kind of angle. She's the witch's daughter, for fuck's sake. I bet Shadow Fire would work on a hellhound."

"I was going to mark Draven anyway, if we couldn't find anything else," I say quietly, my voice hollow. "Maybe she's lying. But maybe she's not. And what she said made sense." Horrifying sense.

Sin lets out a long sigh, rubbing a hand down his face. "Let's try Shadow Fire first. Just once. If that fails, we'll try your suicidal hug-of-death-and-devotion plan."

"We won't get two tries," I say, shaking my head. "The witch already knows we're not going to just roll over and die. She'll expect us to sneak in at the marking ceremony."

"*At least if we die, it will be in the arms of our mate,*" Neris chimes in. "*Silver lining?*"

I almost chuckle. Even now, she hasn't lost her spunk.

I look up at Sin, eyes narrowed with purpose.

"We're not sneaking in."

I roll my shoulders back, heart racing. "We're blowing the damn doors off."

CHAPTER 16

Kassira

"It's time," I tell Sin, locking eyes with him, pretending I'm braver than I feel. The lie tastes bitter.

"*This is going to be such a disaster,*" Neris mutters, ever the cheerful voice of doom.

I ignore her. She's been stuck in a dramatic spiral of *the-end-is-nigh* all week, and honestly? Same. But one of us has to fake composure, and apparently, that job falls to me.

"Shield us. I don't want them feeling us coming until we're already burning the place down," I say, straightening my shoulders.

Sin raises a hand, his shield humming softly around us. "Your wish is my command, Luna Queen," he drawls with a half-hearted grin, but I see the strain tightening around his eyes. The grief hiding behind that false ease.

He hasn't said a word about her — his mate — but he carries the weight in his heart every moment of every day. Unfortunately, there is no time to think about that now. I didn't have time to truly process the danger that my own mate is in, either. We just have to save them first. Survive. And then we'll see what remains.

I draw in a slow breath. "You remember the plan?"

He rolls his eyes, probably exasperated by the fact that this is the hundredth time today alone that I've asked. "There is no real plan, Kass. We go in. I blow shit up. Clear a path for you straight to Draven. We pray they're in the Northern Forest for the ceremony. Otherwise? We're cooked."

"It will be there," I say, a little too quickly. "It's always been there. Every Luna coronation, every royal bond, it's tradition."

Sin snorts but doesn't argue. "I sure hope so," he mumbles and starts walking. "Come on. Clock's ticking. And we don't have any more of Draven's blood to use for teleportation."

We move through the forest in silence. The closer we get to the edge, the heavier my chest feels. By this time tomorrow, we could be rotting in the ground or celebrating our survival.

Gods, I should have told him. I should have told Draven that I love him. That every second with him mattered. I can see the look on his face if I had — those wild stormy eyes lighting up, that crooked, devastating smile taking over his entire face. He'd have scooped me into the sky and demanded I say it again just to hear it through the clouds. I hope it's not too late. I hope I'll still be able to tell him. Back then, it didn't feel like we were living on borrowed time. Not really. Not until he was suddenly gone. Please, let it not be too late.

At least that bitch isn't kissing him anymore. I haven't felt that kind of betrayal through the bond again. But what is she doing to him? He's alone, with her, completely defenseless, and the thought is driving me insane.

Sin suddenly throws his arm in front of me, stopping me in my tracks. His eyes narrow, finger pressed to his lips. I nod, pulse spiking. He heard something. I stretch my senses, but his Alpha hearing is sharper than mine.

A gray wolf steps out of the trees. Black-tipped ears.

He shifts, and there stands Levi. Amira's fucking brother. He grabs a pair of pants hanging from a branch and starts talking.

"I know you're there, Beta. I can smell your magic," he calls out, voice calm and low. He looks in our general direction, but it's clear he can't actually see us.

"Something's wrong at the palace. I've been looking for you for days. All the warriors are under the King's Alpha Command, acting weird. My sister's spreading lies — said the King's true mate cheated on him with you," his gaze cuts toward Sin's general direction, "and that you attacked him in a jealous rage. And now the King is going to mark her. Make her Queen."

He pauses. His jaw clenches.

"I don't know what the hell is happening, but I know when Amira is lying. I don't believe her bullshit about you being a traitor."

His arms cross over his chest, muscles twitching. He

waits, his eyes darting around. "I know something shady and dangerous is going on. The King wouldn't give up on his true mate so easily, I saw them together. I'm guessing you know what's happening and you have a plan. I want to help."

We stand there, frozen.

We should be moving. We should be running. But Sin lifts a hand, stopping me mid-breath, and drops the shield with a flick of his fingers.

"You can smell my magic?" he asks Levi, one brow raised, voice low and sharp.

Levi nods once. No hesitation.

Sin exhales hard, like that answer just confirmed something for him. "You're way past Head Warrior rank, then," he mutters. "You should be aiming for Gamma. Should've kicked Jurgen out a long time ago. Old bastard hasn't smelled a drop of magic in years."

"That's not exactly the priority right now," Levi replies, jaw tense. "Everyone's walking around like enchanted puppets. Even Jurgen. They're all under the King's Command."

My chest tightens. Draven, what is that witch making you do?

"I dodged it," Levi adds, "only because I stayed behind in Mirenwulf for a few days after the funeral. By the time I got back, the palace was crawling with programmed warriors and stories of betrayal. You two are top of the wanted list—" his eyes land on me "—for treason."

"Well," Neris snorts in my head, *"aren't we important."*

I sigh, already tired of this conversation. "Long story short? Your sister and her twin are working with their psychotic witchy birth-mother to steal Draven's power, who happens to be a hellhound, so they can create hellfire and torch the world on behalf of the God of War."

Levi blinks.

And then blinks again.

But I keep going. There's no time for dramatic pauses.

"We need to stop the marking ceremony and break the spell that Draven is under. Tonight is our only chance." I cross my arms, gaze sharp. "So tell me, Levi — how do we know you're not already under the King's command?"

Sin steps up beside me. "I can test him," he offers. "If my Alpha Command lands, it means he's clean."

"I'm fine with that," Levi says with a shrug, chin lifted.

"Alright. But next question — how do we know you're not working with your sister?"

Levi's jaw ticks. His eyes darken.

"First, I'm not a fucking traitor," he snaps. "Second, Amira made my life hell growing up. When I came to the palace for warrior training, I thought I'd finally escaped her. Instead, she followed me here and started fucking my life up again. What was I supposed to do? March up to the King and whine, *'Please, Your Majesty, don't mate the devil incarnate because she used to steal my toys and slap me in front of my friends'*?"

"Draven would've listened," I mumble under my breath. He would have. I know he would have.

"I would've been laughed out of the barracks," Levi grits out. "So I just tried to suck it up."

"Alright, back to business," Sin cuts in, turning toward me. "If he betrays us, I'll burn him to ash."

"Shadow Fire," I add. "Quick and crispy."

Levi pales. "You have Shadow Fire?"

"Yup," Sin says, already walking, hand lifting again to draw the shield around the three of us. "Keep that in mind if you're planning any backstabbing."

"What's the plan then?" Levi asks. "Sneak in, take them down one by one?"

I shake my head. "No sneaking. We go loud. Blast through the Northern entrance mid-ceremony, when they're distracted."

Levi stops dead. We do too.

"You're going the wrong way," he says, face hard. "Amira changed it. Ceremony's in the Southern Garden."

Sin mutters a curse and spins on his heel. "Great. Fantastic. Let's just circle the entire damn kingdom while we're at it." Then he points at Levi, eyes narrow and issues an Alpha Command. "Bark."

"Woof!" Levi scowls, betrayed. "You could've picked literally anything else."

"It was the first thing that came to mind," Sin says without an ounce of shame. "Now run. We've got ground to cover."

"We should shift," Levi grumbles. "Wolves are faster."

"I can't keep the shield up long enough in wolf form," Sin snaps. "So shut up and move."

We listen to the grumpy Beta and pick up the pace.

We stop just outside the high stone wall enclosing the Southern Garden, hidden behind a row of tangled bushes thick enough to hide an army.

"There are people everywhere," I whisper, peeking through the leaves. Movement everywhere. Shadows flitting. Nervous energy coiling through the air.

"Amira chose well," Sin mutters, eyeing the wall. "There's a magical ring around the entire garden. Prevents shifting. No one goes in or out in beast form." He curses under his breath. "Shit. It's rune-based. Old magic. I know it's carved into the perimeter somewhere, but I can't remember where."

My heart stutters. "If you can't shift — if we don't have your dragon — we're screwed."

"You think I don't know that?" he snaps, tension flaring.

Levi's voice cuts through the tight silence. "Wait. So the dragon thing's real? You can actually turn into one?" His wide eyes flick to Sin like he's waiting for him to start breathing fire right at this moment.

Sin doesn't bother answering. Just gives a grim nod.

Levi exhales, then steps closer to the wall, placing his palm against the stone. "I know where some of the runes are. The Gamma used to bring us here for control training — taught us how to fight without shifting, how to leash our beasts." His brow furrows. "I found a few of them while screwing around after hours. If I can take one of the runes out of formation, the whole ring should collapse."

I lean forward. "You're sure?"

He nods. "I can move without suspicion. I'm still part of the royal warriors, after all. I'll signal you when it's done."

"What kind of signal?" I ask.

Levi grins. "Something big. You won't miss it."

"Go," Sin says, voice low and tight. "But if you betray us..." He lifts a single finger. "Shadow Fire."

Levi lifts both hands in mock surrender, eyes dancing. "Yes, Sindre," he says sweetly.

My eyebrows shoot up. "Sindre? That's your full name? The Sparkling One?"

"I will incinerate you both," Sin hisses, deadpan.

"Later," I promise him with a grin. "After we survive."

Sin waves Levi off with a clipped command. "Find the runes. Disrupt the line. And don't get caught."

Levi doesn't hesitate. He vanishes into the garden perimeter like a ghost.

We fall into silence. The kind that's heavy. Breathless. The kind that knows what's coming.

I start to shiver.

"Neris," I whisper inside my mind. *"In case I don't get to say it again... I love you."*

"I love you too, Kass," she murmurs back. *"Not holding my breath, but hey... we do have a habit of surviving the impossible."*

Her tone tries for light. It fails. She's shaking too.

Just a few minutes later, the world moves.

The ground trembles beneath us, a low rumble building into a boom that echoes through the trees. Smoke spirals into the sky, thick and black.

Sin exhales. "That's definitely a signal."

We don't wait.

Within seconds, I'm airborne — clutching white scales and trying not to fall to my death.

Sin's dragon form is massive. Wings like torn parchment, muscles shifting beneath glittering scales. I cling to his mane with one hand, the other holding his sword, too big and heavy to keep it straight.

The moment we cross the garden wall, I release a war cry and hell erupts.

Screams. Fire. Chaos.

Sin roars — a sound ripped from the darkest of nightmares — and unleashes a black blaze so hot it melts through stone like butter. The very air ripples with his fury. Trees bow beneath his wings. Shrubs ignite. Glass shatters.

We cut through the air like a blade, a glowing arc of ash and terror straight toward the center of the garden.

That's where I see them.

Draven and Amira stand in the ruins of what used to be a ceremonial gazebo — now charred wood and shattered stone.

Amira is pacing, panicked, eyes wild.

But Draven... He doesn't move. Doesn't even twitch. His eyes glow a dead, angry red. Hollow. Soulless. Like he's already halfway gone.

The red-headed witch materializes behind him — piecing herself together from his shadow, her hand gripping the leash around his neck like he's her pet. I hate her. I hate her so fucking much.

Just off to the side, leaning lazily against a tree, stands Sinalyn. Sin's mate. Watching everything unfold with glee and... smiling like a lunatic.

I narrow my eyes. This ends today.

For all shifter kind. For the entire Kingdom of Yelora. For the world.

But most of all — for my fucking mate.

CHAPTER 17

Kassira

Sin's dragon crashes into the garden with the force of a natural disaster — wings slicing through air, claws cracking the earth beneath him. The ground shakes. Trees bow. His roar splits the sky open, daring anyone to come closer. No one does.

Everyone's already fled. Everyone but the warriors. The ones still under the King's Command.

"Throw the Shadow Fire!" Sinalyn screams from the edge of the chaos, pointing straight at her mother and sister. "It won't hurt the King!"

"What do you think you're doing, you miserable little worm?" Amira screeches at her.

But the red-headed witch standing behind Draven doesn't move a muscle. Her eyes stay locked on us. Calculating. Cold.

Draven's still motionless. Still hollow.

Sin doesn't wait.

His long neck arches, jaws open wide — and black flame erupts from his throat like a scream of the void. It slams into the ruins of the gazebo, devouring it whole. The witch disappears into Draven's shadow just before the blast hits. Amira dives to the side, barely escaping the inferno.

I leap from Sin's back, land hard — knees jarred, muscles burning — and immediately draw the sword.

The warriors charge. Sin slams his wings wide.

One swing, and a dozen shifters are sent flying like leaves in a storm. He's holding back. I know it. They're not the enemy. Not truly. But they'll keep coming unless something breaks the Command.

Amira comes for me next.

I grip the sword tighter. My whole body wants to shake but I force it still. I'd hoped to land closer to Draven. I can't afford to waste time on her.

"We fight dirty," Neris growls in my head. *"Throw a rock. Kick her in the tits. Blind her with dirt. Anything."*

I don't get the chance.

A blur of gray fur barrels in from the side and slams into Amira mid-run. She flies through the air, crashing into a pillar with a sharp crack. Levi.

He's already after her again, not missing a beat. Oh, perfect. He can handle her.

I run.

Draven. That's all I see. All I care about. Kill him. Mark him. Save him.

I sprint through the garden, weaving between fallen stone and bursts of smoke, sword raised. I'm only a few feet away when the witch reappears from behind him, leash still in hand. Her eyes lock onto mine, and she smiles — a sick twist of mouth and teeth.

She yanks the leash. Draven's head jerks violently, and he moves.

Fast. Too fast.

He catches the blade with his bare hand. Blood drips down the steel, but he doesn't flinch. Just wrenches the sword from my grip and throws it like it's nothing. It clatters uselessly across the stone.

Panic rises in my throat.

The witch bares her teeth. "You're done, little girl," she hisses.

I'm frozen. So close. Too far. Draven's right there. But I can't even touch him.

The world narrows — just me, him, her. The chaos fades. My pulse is thunder in my ears.

"Release him, witch," I growl, teeth clenched.

She tilts her head, mocking. "Or what? What will you do, you weak little wolf? You're powerless." She tightens her grip on the leash even more, squeezing every ounce of hope out of me.

Out of the corner of my eye, I spot Sinalyn — creeping up behind her mother. Silent. Lethal. She meets my eyes and flicks her fingers once.

Keep her talking.

Got it.

I force my voice steady. "So powerless you're too scared to fight me yourself, huh? Thought you'd at least sic the hellhound on me. Guess I overestimated you."

"Ah, ah," the witch singsongs. "You clearly have a plan. You want to get close. But I'm not stupid." She lifts her hand, magic glowing between her fingers. "I don't need the hellhound to kill you. Just a spark. A flick. You'll be ash before your wolf can flick her tail."

"Eager to please your daddy, aren't you?" I spit.

That does it.

Her eyes flare. Rage blooms across her face. "You don't know anything about my father," she growls.

"I know he's a pathetic, bitter little god," I snarl. "Still crying over some battle he lost over two thousand years ago. And the only reason he had you was because he wanted an obedient idiot to carry his wishes without protest." I'm jumping to a lot of conclusions here and making some wild assumptions based on the few pieces of information I've got, but I clearly hit my mark.

She screams — rage and magic building in her throat — and a huge piece of debris explodes near me, shrapnel whistling past my face. I flinch, biting down a scream.

That's when Sinalyn strikes.

She lunges and grips her mother's wrist — the one holding the leash.

Black spreads instantly across the witch's skin, devouring her flesh like rot. She howls, thrashing, but

Sinalyn doesn't let go. She starts dragging her back, away from Draven.

The leash slips from her fingers.

"I can't hold her for long — do it now!" Sinalyn shouts, her voice straining as she wrestles with her mother.

There's no time to hesitate. No space for fear.

"We're using claws, Neris," I whisper. My voice is broken. Like cracked glass.

She doesn't answer — just whimpers and gives them to me. Her claws slide through the tip of my fingers, and I leap. Straight into Draven's chest, arms locked around his shoulders, legs around his waist, holding on like it's the last thing I'll ever do.

He doesn't move. Doesn't sway even a little.

But the second my skin touches his, the world explodes.

Sparks tear through me. His scent wraps around me like a comfort blanket — sun and fire and love. Tears prick instantly at the corners of my eyes. Everything falls silent. The chaos, the fire, the screams. All gone.

It's just us now.

"I love you," I breathe against his ear, voice shaking as my tears spill down his shoulder. "Even if I fail... I won't be far behind."

My lips press to the spot where his neck meets his shoulder — the place where his mark should've always been.

One arm tightens around him. The other raises, claws

out, poised over his chest, fangs descending.

"I'm sorry," I whisper, and then I strike.

My fangs sink into his flesh at the same moment my claws rip through his chest. Right over his heart.

His blood hits my tongue. Not metallic. Not bitter. Sweet. Like wild berries soaked in honey. And gods, the bond hits like lightning.

I feel it open between us — a tunnel, a flare, a scream of light — linking mind to mind, soul to soul. His heart beneath my claws. His blood in my mouth. Everything burns. Magic fights back, dark and violent, but it fails. It dies.

The leash snaps. I feel it unravel.

Marking sigils light up across his skin for a heartbeat, bright and furious.

And then... the light flickers. And fades. The bond dips. And it dies.

I think I hear the witch screaming right when Draven's legs give out and he falls to the ground, taking me with him. My soul is being ripped apart piece by piece, while his soul is already gone.

"No," I sob into his skin, keeping my fangs locked in, refusing to let go even as the pain rips through me like a scythe. I tear my claws from his chest, wrap both arms tight around his neck, and hold.

And hold. And hold.

The world is nothing but absence. His soul is gone. And mine is shattering under the weight of it.

I don't feel anything but pain anymore. I don't even care if I live past this moment. I did everything I could. This was the only way I could fight. I gave everything I had. If he doesn't come back... my twin soul... what use is there in fighting anymore? Who would I keep fighting for?

Neris feels like a raw wound inside my mind, bleeding all over my thoughts. She's howling. We both are. His name, over and over, like a prayer to any god who would listen.

Draven, Draven, Draven.

The pain builds. My mind frays. I don't know how long passes. Time slips away.

Through the agony, I feel a cold hand brushing the top of my head.

"You cry too loud," a dark voice says. Low. Deep. Like a growl buried in shadows. And then, that cold touch is gone.

The next moment, I feel it. A beat. Weak, but there. Inside Draven's chest. And then another one. And another.

I gasp, ripping my fangs from Draven's neck, pressing my ear to his chest.

It's real. It's real. His heart is beating.

I dissolve into sobs, joy and agony mixing into something feral inside of me. My whole body is shaking with it.

His arms suddenly come around me, hugging me

tight. Desperate. Possessive.

My breath leaves me all at once. The pain vanishes like it was never there. And our bond blazes back to life. Not just whole, but unbreakable. Brighter than anything I've ever felt.

"I love you too," he whispers against my skin. That voice. That voice — deep and raw and his. Just like that, I break all over again.

"You heard that?" I sob, the words catching in my throat. Relief floods my entire body. He's back, he's alive.

"It was the only thing that got through," he murmurs. "Your voice."

He pulls back, cradling my face in his hand. Tilts my chin up. His storm-blue eyes are back, full of light. Full of him. No more red.

And there, at the corner of his mouth, is the ghost of a smile.

My mate is back.

"I'll fucking kill you all!" the witch's voice cracks through the air, venom and hate laced in every word.

Shit. I forgot about her.

Draven's smile vanishes in an instant. Silver floods his eyes like moonlight swallowing the night sky. Before I can blink, he's on his feet, lifting me with him. My legs instinctively lock around his waist.

He gives me a kiss. Short, sharp and sweet. Then he sets me down — careful, but fast.

My gaze instantly drops to his chest. Nothing. No dark

bruise. No sign of the wound I carved there to bring him back. Just perfect, unmarred skin. I want to see *my* mark, my name seared into him, but he's too damn tall.

All the air leaves my lungs when his wings explode from his back. Massive, blinding and on fucking fire!

"What the hell, Draven? You're on fire!" I shout, stumbling back.

He smirks. Dark. Dangerous. Like he knows what he's become.

"Yeah, I am," he says, voice like velvet. Then with a single sweep of his hand, a circle of fire bursts to life around me. Waist-high flames that crackle and dance like they're alive.

"My fire won't hurt you," he murmurs, eyes flicking over me. "But it'll burn everything and everyone else. Stay inside the ring, Kassira. Don't move. I need you safe."

I keep my mouth shut. Let him do his thing. I'll gladly watch from my privileged position.

I nod once and let him go. Watch him walk into battle like the king he was born to be.

My legs wobble. My hands tremble. But I keep my eyes on him. I'm not going to miss a second.

Around us, the battlefield seethes. Sin is still fending off the warriors, blowing through them like a hurricane. Levi's locked in his own brawl — pinning Amira while trying to keep two others off his back. It's chaos. It's carnage.

Draven looks around once and then he roars.

A sound so deep, so loud, so violent that it shakes the ground. Debris launches into the air. Trees rattle. Warriors drop to their knees instantly, heads bowed, foreheads to the dirt.

All of them. Even Levi. Even Amira. Except Sin. Of course not Sin. I don't know why the hell that is, but one day I'll figure it out.

Satisfied, Draven turns his gaze to the red-headed witch. She's chanting now, fast and frantic, her hands glowing with weak crimson threads.

Neris yips inside my head, tail wagging like a maniac. *"Our mate's back, Kass! He's really back! And he's gonna burn that bitch."*

I sure hope so.

The witch throws a bolt of red lightning at him. He doesn't even dodge it. Just keeps walking like she's throwing pieces of paper. She hurls another one toward me — it hits the ring of hellfire and disintegrates on impact.

She looks terrified now. That's right, you evil witch. Your time's up.

My eyes flick to the side. I see poor Sinalyn slumped against a tree, chest rising slowly. I hope she's ok. Without her, we wouldn't be standing right now.

A surge of excitement and pure pleasure goes through me when Draven shifts into Draxis mid-step. Without a lick of hesitation. Without breaking his stride for even one moment. One blink, and there's no more man. Just the monster. The beast. Ten feet of nightmare. Wings ablaze. Scales gleaming under his fur. Eyes molten silver.

Neris freezes, eyes fixed on him. I freeze too, watching with bated breath.

He stops a few feet from the witch and raises one clawed hand. Just a flick of the wrist.

Golden fire ignites at her feet.

She screams — high, sharp and inhuman. She tries to run. The flames follow. She tries to stamp them out. They surge higher.

They eat her alive.

I watch, eyes wide, throat dry. Her skin blackens. Then sloughs off. Her shrieks cut into the sky, and still Draxis watches calmly. Cold. Like a god judging the damned.

The stench hits me next. Burned rot. Boiled flesh. I gag and cover my mouth with my hand.

Neris doesn't look away once. She's watching the witch being eaten alive by hellfire like it's a theater play.

Finally, she collapses. A twitching pile of burnt meat and ash. But Draxis doesn't stop.

The hellfire consumes her. Her bones. Her magic. Everything. Until there's nothing left. Not even dust.

I squeak when a man materializes in front of Draxis, cloaked in golden armor, soaked in blood, a warhammer clutched in his hand. He stands where the witch once burned, the nothing she became now a void between them.

It can't be... That can't be... No, no, he can't be here!

"Aresssss," Draxis hisses, his voice a broken growl.

Shit, of course. The God of War is here. Because his daughter just died.

Ares sighs, and looks at the empty space where the witch used to be, seeming unbothered. "Did you really have to burn her soul, too?"

Draxis lifts a single talon and flames start building back up, violent and alive, heat thickening the air. The fire builds fast and Ares takes a sharp step back, instinct flaring. Then the mad bastard laughs. Head thrown back, chest shaking.

"Come on now," Ares says, all smug ease and slick charm. "You know how it is — love and war, no rules." He flashes Draxis a grin like they're old friends meeting for drinks instead of standing over the ashes of his dead daughter.

Draxis growls low in his throat. The sound is pure warning. He's not amused.

Ares raises his hands in mock surrender. "Alright, alright. Believe it or not…" He clears his throat, a flicker of discomfort passing over his face. "I may have… forgotten about this little plan of mine. Thanatos clued me in on what was going down." His gaze flicks to the scorched earth between them. "I actually came to stop it before things got out of hand. But," he shrugs, jaw ticking, "looks like I was too late."

Draxis narrows his eyes, clearly not believing him and sends another burst of hellfire at the god. Ares' previously charming smile instantly twists into something ugly and cruel. His red eyes flash with hunger for battle. I swear the world holds its breath.

"Hellhound," Ares sneers, cracking his neck,

warhammer glinting in the moonlight. "You're not even a god. You're a weapon that forgot its place. Be careful of your next step."

Draxis doesn't answer. He growls, a low sound that starts deep in his chest and ripples through the ground beneath my feet. Fire bursts in twin trails down his spine, smoke rising from where the talons on his feet curl into the earth.

And then he lunges.

Faster than thought, he's on Ares, jaw snapping for the god's throat. But Ares twists, swings his warhammer in a brutal arc. It slams into Draxis's ribs with a crack that shatters trees in the distance. Draxis roars, wings of fire flaring wide, and uses the momentum to slam his talons into Ares' side. Sparks explode as metal meets bone.

They collide again, like storms clashing, the sound louder than thunder.

Ares slams a fist into Draxis's face, sending him crashing into a stone pillar. I scream, heart clawing up my throat. The pillar crumbles around Draxis, but before the dust even settles, he is up, charging through the rubble, his eyes glowing silver, his fury almost a living thing.

He tackles the god into the ground with unbelievable speed.

Claws sink into golden armor. Metal bends. Blood pours. Ares laughs like a crazy person.

"You think rage makes you strong?" he snarls, twisting beneath Draxis, driving his elbow into his throat. "I am rage made flesh."

Draxis howls, a sound that fractures the air. He bites down on Ares' shoulder, fangs sinking deep enough to pierce muscle. Ares stops laughing. He's screaming now.

But he doesn't stay down. He channels his power, his body glowing with a radiant, red pulse. It blasts Draxis off him, flinging him through the air like a ragdoll. He crashes into a huge marble statue, wings trailing sparks.

"Kneel!" Ares roars, his warhammer spinning in his grip, red fire spiraling up the shaft.

Draxis gets up and steps forward, blood staining the dirt. His body shakes.

"I said kneel!"

Draxis lifts his head. His voice, when it comes, is low. Raw.

"Only forrr maattteee," he growls and then he launches himself at the god.

They clash again.

Ares laughs — until Draxis carves through his armor, blood splattering the dirt.

Until my magnificent hellhound shoves one hand against the god's chest — and burns.

Hellfire ignites.

The battlefield turns white-hot. Ares screams, flames curling around his body, licking at his flesh.

His golden armour melts. Holy shit. My mate is melting a god!

Draxis slams Ares down, fangs bared.

"Forrr my mattteeee," he snarls, voice shaking the skies. "Forrr everrry scrrream of herrrss. Forrr everrry tearrr. Forrrr the chainsss you helped forrrge." The words are broken, cracked, but they're clear. And they make my heart soar.

He opens his jaws wide, hellfire glowing inside his throat, and lets it erupt.

Ares is engulfed.

When the fire fades, the god lies broken, scorched into the earth. The next second, he's gone. Disappears.

And Draxis — bloody and furious — lifts his head to the sky and howls.

A war cry. A promise. If the god ever comes back, he won't be able to leave again.

"Wow." The whisper comes from my right and nearly sends me flying out of my own skin. I whip around, heart in my throat.

Sin stands next to me, cradling an unconscious Sinalyn in his arms. His eyes are locked on Draxis, reverence painted across every inch of his face.

"When the hell did you get here?" I hiss, still clutching my chest.

He tears his gaze away from Draxis just long enough to glance at me. "A while ago," he says, as if that explains anything, then turns on his heel and walks off, carrying his mate like she weighs nothing.

I barely have time to breathe before another voice cuts through the air.

"I'm here, too." Levi. I spin, nerves shot. I'm going to strangle the next person who sneaks up on me.

He stands behind me, looking completely unfazed, holding a very bloody, very broken Amira by the arm. Her head is bowed, her posture trembling. She's barely conscious, barely upright.

"She's still alive?" I ask, blinking in surprise.

He shrugs, unbothered. "It's the King and Queen's place to punish her."

"*I agree with him!*" Neris chirps, her tail swishing. "*I've already got a few fun ideas!*"

Her giddiness makes me chuckle.

The flames encircling me begin to flicker and die, retreating into nothing.

I turn and see Draxis walking toward me, power and purpose in every step. He shifts mid-stride, the transformation smooth, instinctive, as natural to him now as breathing. After all the trouble we've gone through with trying to make him shift, he's doing it now like he's done it his entire life. His body gleams with strength, not a single scratch left behind.

My heart cracks wide open.

I don't wait for him to reach me. I run straight into his arms.

He doesn't hesitate, he lifts me off the ground in an instant, burying his face in the crook of my neck, his strong arms holding me tightly.

His voice rumbles against my skin as he shifts me

slightly in his hold, peering over my shoulder. "The dungeon," he commands. "We'll deal with her later."

And then his fiery wings blaze to life — black bone laced in living hellfire, the flames dancing along the edges like they were born to kiss the sky. I lean into him and he takes off through the air.

CHAPTER 18

Draven

She smells like earth and defiance and everything I fought to come back to.

"I thought I lost you," she whispers, shivering slightly.

"You did," I breathe, voice low. "But you called me back."

We shatter into the sky, the earth falling away, the clouds parting like silk. She's cradled against my chest, arms wrapped around my neck, her heartbeat steady.

The higher we go, the more the world fades.

I level us out, coasting high above the forest and mountains in the distance. The wind whips around us, but the heat from my wings keeps her warm. All the events of today — of the last few days, of the last years — fade away. It's only her that matters. Only this moment.

My hand slides behind her neck, pulling her forehead to mine. "You saved me. You brought me back when even I didn't believe I could come back. You're mine, Kassira. I'm never letting you go," I say, voice rough.

Her breath catches.

I press my lips to hers — soft at first, then deeper, until her fingers are fisting my hair, her body melting into mine midair. My wings flare wide, the fire pulsing with each beat of my heart.

Her scent is tangled in my skin now, woven into every breath I take. Her mark sings through my veins, each beat of my heart screaming her name. And yet I'm still starving for her.

I draw back just enough, mouth brushing her jaw. The second I pull back slightly and our eyes lock, I snap. I can't hold myself back anymore.

She marked me to save my life. Now I'll mark her to claim hers.

She knows what's coming. I can see it in her eyes. The raw, wild need that matches mine.

I tilt her head with one hand and bare her throat with the other.

She doesn't resist.

Her pupils are blown wide, her lips parted, chest rising fast as her body presses harder into mine.

There's no thought left.

I lower my head to the curve of her neck and feel her pulse against my mouth.

The bond thrums between us, tense, bright and desperate.

I bare my fangs. Her pulse flutters against my lips.

I bite hard, maybe harder than I need to. Her blood floods my mouth and it's so intoxicating that I close my eyes in pleasure.

As my fangs sink in, her soul flares like sunlight, her body arching in my arms. Her cry splits the wind. My fire responds, flames from my wings snapping outward in a blaze of gold and red and pure light.

The bond slams into place. Complete and unbreakable.

Magic erupts from us — mine and hers — melding like molten steel, searing across her skin in glowing sigils only I can read. They shine for a heartbeat, etched into her flesh like a vow.

Her mark forms across the base of her neck and shoulder. My name, forever on her skin.

And then I feel hers. I couldn't feel it when she marked me, I was lost to the curse. But now it tears through me like lightning. Her soul claims me back, a silken chain of starlight wrapping around my heart.

I groan against her skin, holding her tighter than I thought I ever could.

We're falling — weightless, slow, not down, but into each other.

Into forever.

I pull back, lips brushing her ear.

"You're mine now," I whisper.

She smiles.

"That doesn't mean you're off the hook for all these mate problems you brought into my life."

We laugh as hellfire dances behind us, lighting the night sky like a second sun.

I kiss her like she's the air I need to breathe. Like if I stop, I'll forget how to exist.

She moans against my mouth, grinding into me with a hunger that sends a dangerous spark shooting down my spine. Her scent wraps around me like silk.

"I need you, Your Majesty," she whispers, her voice low, a plea masked as a challenge.

My grip tightens on her hips, dragging her closer, chest to chest, her warmth burning through every layer of me.

"Call me 'Your Majesty' again," I growl against her throat, kissing a trail down her skin. "And I'll ruin you, right here, midair."

She arches back, smug and sinful. "Your Majesty," she breathes, and the sound of it — sweet and sharp and teasing — makes something primal inside me rise to the surface.

I growl deep in my chest, shifting her effortlessly, her legs wrapping tighter around my waist. My mouth finds hers again, slower now, deeper. The kind of kiss that tastes like forever.

Her shirt comes apart with just one swipe of my claw, and she gasps, startled. But there's laughter in it, and raw need in her eyes. Her breasts spill into the open, nipples pebbling instantly from the wind. She leans into me, daring me to lose control.

She trembles in my arms, breath catching as I bring my hand down her back, dragging my fingers along her spine. The sounds she makes drive me half-mad. I tilt her hips against mine and she gasps again, arching into me, lips parting in anticipation.

Our magic hums between us, the bond flaring wild in the space where our skin meets.

The need for her grows impossibly higher inside of me. I kiss her again and she groans against my lips, lost to the moment.

The last shred of control that I was still clinging to starts cracking, fraying at the edges.

One second, she's kissing me — taunting me with that wicked mouth, grinding against me like sin incarnate — and the next, her pants are gone. Torn by my claws clean through the middle. No hesitation. No mercy.

She gasps, breathless and smiling. That maddening, beautiful smile of hers that always makes me forget everything.

"That was my favorite pair," she tries, voice mock-wounded, even as her fingers dig deeper into my shoulders.

I growl low in my chest, the sound dark and possessive. "I'll buy you a thousand more," I promise, voice rough and filled with desire.

I lean her back, her spine arching like a bow, her perfect breasts completely exposed to me.

Her fingers slide into my hair, grip tightening at the back of my head as she pulls me forward — letting me know exactly what she needs. I tease one of her hardened nipples with the tip of a claw before bringing my mouth down and catching it between my teeth, biting hard enough to make her yelp, then soothe it with my tongue. A groan filled with pleasure slips from her lips and a full-body shiver ripples through her.

I grip the curves of her ass with both hands, dragging her hard against me, grinding her soaked heat along the length of my cock. She's drenched — her need slick and desperate, leaving no question about what she wants. I bite her nipple and suck, a growl vibrating in my chest, and tighten my hold, fingers digging deep into her flesh.

I slide a hand up her spine, anchoring her to me, pressing her chest to mine until I can feel the frantic beat of her heart against my ribs. Then I sink two fingers into her pussy from behind — slow, deep and unrelenting. She whimpers, grinding harder against me, her breath catching on a moan. I smile against her throat and drag my fangs over the mark I carved into her skin, biting down just enough to make her shiver.

But the moment her teeth sink into my own fresh mark, a jolt of brutal, blinding pleasure rips through me.

And that's it. The last thread of restraint snaps.

My cock aches to be inside of her, to push deep into her wet core.

I thrust into her in one savage, fluid motion, my wings flaring wide, sending the clouds around us scattering like smoke. She cries out my name, head thrown back, voice wrecked with pleasure. I don't wait. I don't ease her in. I fuck her like I've been dying to — hard, fast, desperate. My hands grip her hips, guiding her along my cock, her body stretching around me like she was made for this.

She's perfection — falling apart in my arms, breathless, gasping, begging without words. Each time I drive into her, her walls clamp down tighter, slick and pulsing, milking me for everything I've got. My balls tighten and pleasure licks up my spine, white hot lightning blazing at the base. It's building like a storm that's about to crack the sky wide open. Fast, furious and inevitable.

Her pussy tightens around my cock, gripping me in a way that makes my breath hitch. I know she's close to the edge. I can see it. Every roll of my hips makes her tremble harder, her nails dragging across my skin, leaving scratches that vanish the second they're made.

I feel the exact moment when she breaks. Her breath catches. Her whole body seizes. Her eyes lock on mine — wide, silent, undone. I don't stop. I can't. I move her faster, needing to feel every inch of her wrapped around me. I crush my mouth to hers, devouring her lips with feral hunger and when I bite down, it's just shy of breaking skin. I bury my cock to the hilt inside of her, over and over again until I feel her breaking for a second time and I shatter with her, a deafening roar ripping out of my chest. My cum coats her pussy, dripping down her thighs, branding my scent into her.

I groan softly against her lips and drop my forehead to her shoulder, locking my arms around her. Her heartbeat drums wild and fast against my chest. It's a sound I never want to stop hearing.

"I want this to be at least a weekly thing," she whispers, her breath brushing against the shell of my ear.

I huff a laugh, amused. "That's a no from me. We're definitely doing this several times a day."

She chuckles — warm and smug — and the sound goes straight to my cock, igniting the hunger all over again.

"I meant the *'in the air'* part, you Royal Pain in the Ass."

I grin, teeth flashing, voice dipping lower. "I'll show you pain in the ass one of these days," I growl against her skin, dragging my lips along the curve of her neck. "But for now," I say and start moving inside her again, "it seems that we're not done."

Her sigh filled with need curls through me like sin brought to life.

CHAPTER 19

Draven

"What do you want to do with her?" I ask Kass, voice calm, almost bored.

We're in the Royal Hall. The entire court watches in heavy silence, tension hanging thick in the air. I'm slouched on my throne, one arm draped lazily over the side, while Kass sits beside me — my Luna Queen. Her eyes gleam with satisfaction as they rest on Amira, who kneels on the stone floor below. Wrists shackled, head bowed.

It's been a week since the battle. Since Kass broke the leash and brought me back. We already had our official ceremony, making her the Luna Queen of all shifters. Of course, we had to do a pretend marking in front of the Alphas of the six Prime Packs and their representatives. But that wasn't unusual. Many royal pairings have done it like this before. True mates can rarely keep themselves from marking each other as soon as possible.

Of course, our situation was much different, though. There were questions. A lot of them. Kass and I shared the details with the Alpha Primes and the Council — it's important for them to be informed about this kind of shit.

Everyone was baffled. No witch has done anything of these proportions since the Witch-Shifter Wars. And that was hundreds of years ago. Fortunately, this time it was just one witch and her daughters — not an entire faction of them. Well, and a stupid god who got his ass kicked. I'll be reporting that asshole to the gods who rule the Kingdom of Solmere. The ones who protect our entire realm. Let's see how he deals with two angry Primordial gods who outrank him in every way.

I feel a peace inside me, the kind I've never felt before. Draxis and Neris also marked each other the same day Kass and I did. It was fun. Neris made Draxis work for it. She kept running and hiding in these tiny holes in the forest where only she could fit — Draxis had to dig her out every time. He indulged her playfulness for a while, until he lost his patience and caught her in two seconds flat.

"Well, Neris has ideas," Kass answers my previous question, a wicked glint in her eyes.

I grin. Of course she does. That little wolf is more bloodthirsty than Draxis. "Oh yeah?"

Kass claps her hands together, eyes sparkling. She's just as bloodthirsty as her wolf — she just doesn't like to admit it. "Word for word: *'Claws through the heart. Rip it out. Burn it. Then burn the whole body with hellfire. No funeral for her.'*"

She pauses, then adds innocently, "She wants Draxis to do it. Says she's been dreaming of this moment."

I rise to my feet, stretch, and crack my knuckles. "Well, far be it from me to deny my mate her dream."

Amira lifts her head slowly, tears streaking her cheeks. "Please," she croaks. "Ven—Draven, please. I never meant to… she made me. Galla forced me. I—I loved you."

I blink once. "Liar." My voice is colder than ice.

"You really want to beg? Here? After everything? You could've at least owned it. Died with a shred of dignity."

She opens her mouth again, but I don't care to hear more. I need this settled fast. I've got a *make-up-for-being-a-problem-magnet* date with my mate after this.

I let Draxis take over. He bursts forward in a flurry of torn fabric. Shit. I forgot about my clothes.

His claws click against the stone floor and his wings stretch, but there's no fire this time. We can't risk burning the whole palace down. I feel his joy. His anticipation.

He stalks toward Amira slowly, purposefully, snarling low in his throat. Drool drips from his maw. Amira shakes violently. If she wasn't shackled, she'd be trying to run.

When he's close, he snaps his jaw inches from her face. She screams, lurching back, chains rattling against the floor. I chuckle. He really likes amping up the drama.

Draxis huffs.

He's done playing.

The bond between Kass and me surges, her satisfaction humming along it. When Draxis lifts one massive claw and drives it into Amira's chest, I feel Kass's heartbeat stutter in delight.

Draxis doesn't waste any more time. He does exactly as Neris instructed. Amira screams so loud that my ears ring. He only has to pull at her chest once to rip her heart out. One clean, precise strike. And then he lifts her heart from her chest like a trophy, blood steaming in the open air, and turns toward Kass — presenting it like an offering, snarling proudly.

Her smile could bring kingdoms to their knees.

"Thank you, Draxis," she says sweetly, sending him a wink and blowing a kiss.

Okay. Hold the fuck up. I'm here, too.

"Our mate likes me more," Draxis throws at me, smug as hell.

"Dream on, you overgrown mutant," I shoot back.

He huffs a laugh and turns back to the task at hand. Flames lick up from his claws like serpents. The entire room takes two instinctive steps back.

He incinerates the heart first. Lets it burn to a crisp before tossing it onto what's left of Amira. The fire flares, devouring everything she was. Flesh. Bone. Even the scent.

When it's done, I reclaim control and shift.

"Assembly's over," I call out flatly, scanning the stunned faces in the Royal Hall. "You can leave now."

Chairs scrape. Boots shuffle. The court disperses fast.

I turn to Kass.

She's lounging on her throne, smiling at me. Smug.

Beautiful. Mine.

"You look like you've got something to complain about," she teases, arching a brow.

I stalk toward her, eyes locked on her mouth. When I reach her, I tug her up, press my lips to hers and kiss her slow. Deep.

"Not bothered by my nudity anymore, are you?" I murmur against her mouth.

She shrugs, biting her lip like she's trying not to laugh. "I've grown accustomed to your Royal jewels." Her tone is light, but that sparkle in her eyes? Dangerous.

I chuckle. "Strange. Shifters are used to nudity. We live half our lives bare. You should've been used to this by now."

She tilts her head, thoughtful. "I grew up pretty isolated. Not many pack runs, not many naked shifters running around. Maybe that's why." Her gaze narrows. She presses a finger to the center of my chest. "But don't get any ideas. Just because shifters are used to nudity doesn't mean your... assets get to be public domain. Those Royal jewels? They're mine. Keep them away from wandering eyes."

I bark out a laugh. "Possessive, aren't you?" I nip her nose and let the grin drop from my face. "But noted. I'll respect your wishes."

I glance down at myself. "Now I just need to find a damn pair of pants, so we can leave this room."

She strolls back to her throne, casual as ever, and picks up a neatly folded pair from the side.

"Already handled. Sent someone the moment Draxis shredded yours," she says and throws them at me.

I smile, holding them to my chest. "Have I told you I love you today?"

She plants a hand on her hip, lips twitching. "You have. But feel free to say it again."

I dress quickly, eyes never leaving her.

"I love you, Kass. More than anything and anyone."

She walks toward me, warmth shining in her eyes. "And I love you too," she says and pauses for a second, "Your Majesty," she adds playfully, making me growl softly. Then she grins. "Now… what are our plans for the rest of the day?"

Two weeks later, I'm pacing the ballroom floor — waiting for Kass to show up. I'm on pins and needles. I don't know if this was the right thing to do. My boots echo against the marble, my heart beating like it's trying to claw its way out of me.

This might've been a mistake.

Maybe she won't want the reminder.

What if she hates it?

What if she hates *me* for doing this? Shit. I almost stop

breathing at the thought.

"*Our mate is generous and kind,*" Draxis murmurs, exasperated. "*She won't hate us. And she'll understand.*"

"You don't know that," I snap back.

He huffs, unimpressed. "*And you call me dramatic. Get it together, human. If she bolts, I'll just hunt her down and chain her to our bed.*"

I freeze mid-step. "You will do no such thing!" I hiss. "She'd decapitate us in our sleep. Worst case scenario, we just lock her in a nice, big room and give her lots and lots of books and food. Until she calms down," I say, weighing my options.

"You are so whipped," Sin mutters from behind, his voice dripping with judgment and just a hint of amusement.

I glare over my shoulder. "Appreciate the moral support."

He shrugs. "I just call it like I see it."

I open my mouth to retaliate — but the words never make it out.

Because she walks in. And I forget how to breathe.

Kass steps through the grand doors, Sinalyn trailing at her side. I barely register the witch. My gaze locks on my mate.

A deep green dress hugs her curves like sin. Her hair spills over one shoulder, loose and soft, begging for my hands. She glows.

"*Move, you idiot,*" Draxis snarls, practically shoving me

forward from inside my mind. *"Go to our mate."*

My feet unfreeze. I cross the floor like I'm caught in a spell, meeting her halfway. She smiles at me, genuine and bright.

"Why are you so nervous, Draven?" she asks, a hint of amusement in her voice. "I could feel you going crazy through the bond for the past hour."

Shit. Right. That whole shared feelings thing.

I scan the tether between us — searching for any trace of reluctance on her part. There's nothing but calm. Curiosity. Contentment.

I exhale and lift a hand to her cheek, brushing her skin with my thumb. Her warmth grounds me.

"This is where we first met," I whisper.

Her eyes widen slightly, flicking around the ballroom. I feel the recognition settle inside her. But no shadows follow it.

I take a breath and let the rest spill out.

"I can't undo what happened that night. I can't rip it out of time and pretend it didn't exist. But I can try to give you something else. New, better memories." I step in closer, my forehead almost brushing hers. "Let me rewrite that night, Kass. Let me gift you a new first meeting. The one that should have been all along."

For a moment, she says nothing.

Then her smile stretches. "It's a gift for you too, isn't it?" she teases gently, resting her palm over my heart. "I accept."

She steps back, eyes gleaming. And just like that night, she says it again.

"You're my mate."

"What did you just say?" I ask, repeating my own words.

She lifts her chin, defiant. "You're my mate."

I grin, stepping into her space, winding an arm around her waist.

"You're damn right I am," I growl, voice echoing through the ballroom for everyone to hear.

EPILOGUE 1

Sinalyn

It shouldn't hurt this much. Not for a witch. Not for me.

Galla's words were all lies and I should have known better. She told me so many things, but only when they served her own purpose. I don't know why I believed her about this. After everything she did to me.

When she spoke about mates, she made me think it didn't feel the same for us as it does for shifters. It was never supposed to be this intense. This powerful. Nothing like the searing pain in my heart. That's why she always said rejection is simple for witches. A bond so loose, so meaningless — it comes easy and leaves without leaving a scratch.

But the constant sharp, piercing pain inside my chest is proof of her lies. And my mate didn't even reject me. Not yet, at least.

I press my palm against my chest, trying to breathe through the agony of being near him but suffering his hate. The pressure inside me keeps building up and one day I'm sure it will explode.

I have to stay here for the next year. A whole year. It's a long time to stay when he hates me this much already. But I promised the Luna Queen I'd help her with her old magic research. Until she knows all she needs to. I owe it to her — she could have easily asked the King to kill me. Instead, she protected me and gave me a place here. And I desperately need my own answers about the sigil that Galla put on me, too. I have a chance to find the truth in the Royal Archives. To finally know what she did to me.

Dammit. Why did I have to have a mate? Only a third of witches, at most, have one. After everything I went through — after everything Galla put me through — the gods could have at least granted me this one small mercy of not suffering like this. Not having to feel this pain.

I splash some water over my face, trying to keep myself together. It was sweet what the King did for the Queen tonight. Exactly the type of thing I will never have. But having to be so close to my mate all night, it broke another piece of me. Every time he turned those green, hateful eyes my way, it felt like he was driving his sword straight through my heart.

I pat my face with a soft towel and leave the restroom. I've been in here long enough. I need to get myself together.

But I don't make it two steps when strong arms pin me to the wall. And those green eyes that have been following me all night are now locked on me. Closer. Hotter. Still hateful. Still angry. Still breaking me in half.

"What the fuck are you still doing here," he hisses, voice furious.

I try to wiggle out of his hold, but he won't budge. "It

has nothing to do with you. Please let me go," I whisper.

"It has everything to do with me," he snarls. "Do you think that if you hang around here, throwing yourself in my space like some slut, I might accept you? It will never happen. You might have fooled Kass and Draven, but you can't fool me."

My throat closes up. My body is shivering now, the pain inside me flaring to impossible heights. "What are you talking about?" I ask him, my voice soft and quiet.

"I'm talking about the fact that you're just as rotten as your mother and sister. The only reason you helped us was because you saw the end coming and wanted to save your ass," he growls.

The hatred in his voice makes me shiver harder. I feel a tear rolling down my cheek.

He steps back suddenly, like I burned him.

"Stop the act," he says, voice cold. "I can smell the deceit and death hanging off you. Your tears are just as fake as the rest of you." He leans forward, voice getting even colder. "Leave the palace or you'll end up dead."

With those parting words, he turns around and leaves me alone in the dark hallway, drowning in misery and pain.

EPILOGUE 2

Kassira

"**I**'m going to kick his royal ass," I mutter under my breath, storming down the corridor — the one that finally got patched up after Sin's dragon blew a hole clean through it over three months ago. Mental note — kick the Beta's ass, too. He needs to stop brooding and claim his damn mate already.

But first — my mate.

I shove open the Council War Room doors without knocking. Nine pairs of eyes snap to me in stunned silence.

"Draven," I growl.

His eyes flash with amusement. He probably thinks I sound like an angry kitten. Cute. Let's see how cute I am when I claw his pretty face off.

"Out," he commands, voice clipped. The Council scatters in less than two seconds. Impressive.

Sin saunters past me, casual confidence in every step.

"Don't maim him too bad," he drawls with a smirk. "We still need to finish the meeting."

"You're next, wonder boy," I snap, shooting daggers at him.

His eyes go comically wide, and without another word, he bolts. Levi trails behind him, calm and composed.

"Luna," Levi greets with a respectful nod.

"Gamma," I purr, syrup-sweet. He's a good egg. Doesn't deserve my wrath — yet.

Then I turn back to Draven and glare daggers at his handsome face.

He smiles. That lazy, indulgent smile that always makes me want to kiss him silly — just not this time. He takes a step toward me.

I raise a hand to stop him but he doesn't. Not until my palm presses to the hard wall of his chest. I grip his shirt and yank, forcing him closer.

"I'm very unhappy, mate," I say quietly, teeth clenched.

His smile drops. A low growl rumbles from his chest, vibrating straight into my bones.

"What happened? Who do I kill?" His voice is deeper now, raw. Draxis is bleeding through.

Neris sighs in my mind. *"Normally, I would be all for seeing Draxis in action, but you are way too dramatic right now, Kass."*

"*Shut up, Neris. This is a crisis,*" I hiss.

I tilt my chin up and glare harder.

"Why the hell am I not allowed in my own library?" I demand. "I had a meeting with Aly this morning, and a guard stopped me at the door. Said it was on your orders!"

Draven blinks, surprised. Then he grins and his eyes light up. "That's why you're mad?"

"It's not funny!" I snap, tightening my grip on his shirt. "The guard said to come talk to you!"

He chuckles and pulls me against him, wrapping his arms around my waist. Like I'm not a threat. Like I'm not seconds away from committing regicide.

"I didn't think you'd be up this early," he murmurs, brushing a kiss to the tip of my nose. "You were up late last night. I figured you'd sleep in. The library's closed because I'm having something prepared for you. It'll be ready in an hour."

Excitement flares in my chest, cutting through the outrage. "Really?" I ask, brows lifting. "What kind of surprise?"

"You'll see soon, my beautiful mate," he says, smug as hell. "Now — did you eat?"

"Yes," I huff. "Oh, and the cook told me to tell you that we have enough deer meat to feed the entire kingdom for the next five years. Draxis can relax now. I won't be starving anytime soon."

Draven's eyes darken with heat. "We'll find something else to hunt for you," he rumbles, low and dangerous.

A shiver races down my spine.

He grins like he felt it himself and he backs me up until my spine hits the door I just kicked in. I hear the click of the lock behind me, and my breath stutters.

"What are you doing, Draven?" I whisper, throat dry, voice thick.

He leans in, crowding me, his lips hovering just over mine.

"You're irresistible when you're angry," he murmurs, and his mouth claims mine with a desperate hunger.

I moan into the kiss, arms winding around his neck, body molding to the hard lines of him. My skirt tangles around my hips as he hikes me up, pinning me between the door and the heat of his body.

His hands are everywhere — palming my ass, sliding up my thighs, kneading the muscle with rough, possessive force. His claws drag along my bare skin, just enough to sting. I gasp, arching into him. He loves it. I can feel his need spark through our bond, stoking mine even higher.

The world outside the door dissolves. There is only this — his teeth at my throat, the scrape of fangs at my jaw, me grinding against him until I'm shaking and desperate.

"You could have just told me about the library," I pant, biting his lower lip when he tries to speak.

He rumbles deep in his chest, the vibration making my toes curl. "But then I wouldn't get to see you like this. Wild and furious. My favorite version of you."

He grabs my wrists, pins them above my head with one hand, and yanks my shirt open with the other. I shiver as the cooler air hits my skin, nipples pebbling under his gaze. His tongue traces the edge of my mark, and I can't help the whine that escapes me.

"Mine," he growls, and sinks his teeth in gently — just enough to remind me of the truth written over my skin.

"Yes, yes, yours. Now stop playing," I gasp, writhing against him. He lets go of my wrists, and my hands immediately tangle in his hair, dragging him closer. Demanding more.

His hands are under my skirt, claws snagging the lace of my underwear. He rips them off in a single, savage pull. The move is so primal, so utterly him, that for a moment I can't breathe. He shoves my skirt up, exposing me completely, and his fingers slide between my thighs, slick with need. He teases me, thumb circling my clit, two fingers sliding deep inside me. Curling. I nearly scream.

"I'll never get enough of this," he rasps, watching me fall apart on his hand. "Never get tired of seeing you come undone for me."

I don't last long. Not with the way he moves, not with the way he owns every inch of my body. I claw at his arms, my head thrown back against the door. When I shatter, I see stars. I see him — my mate — haloed in fire.

He doesn't wait for me to recover. He lets me down and spins me around, palms flat against the door.

"Do you want me fuck you, my Luna?" he growls, voice so deep it vibrates between my legs, sending a new jolt of pleasure. His fingers brush the curve of my ass, a touch so filled with heat that it's a miracle I don't combust instantly.

"As if you even need to ask," I manage, voice barely a breath.

He laughs, low and deep. "Say it," he commands, darkness slipping into his voice, amusement gone.

"Fuck me, Draven," I whisper, and the effect is immediate.

I brace myself, heart pounding, breath ragged. I hear the sound of his zipper, the slap of his cock against my ass. And then he's inside me. One hard, deep thrust that makes my vision go white.

He fills me, stretches me, and there's no gentleness in the way he takes me. Possessive. Fierce. The way I like it. His hands clamp my hips, dragging me back to meet each savage thrust. My cheek presses to the wood, breath fogging in frantic bursts. Every time he slams into me, my body sings with pleasure.

"Say it again," he rasps, voice raw, lips curved in a hungry grin. "Say you're mine."

"I'm yours," I gasp, nails raking the heavy door until splinters dig into my skin. Each thrust makes the world narrow, makes the bond between us flare — hot and bright and so strong it hurts. I feel him everywhere inside of me.

He shifts his angle, hits that spot, and I nearly sob.

"Draven, please—"

He laughs, low and dark. "You're so fucking greedy," he groans.

His hand snakes up to wrap around my throat, pulling

me upright against his chest. His other hand moves down, finds my clit, and circles it in a rough, perfect rhythm to the pounding of his cock. My knees buckle, but he holds me up, body caged by his, every muscle tensed around me.

The pleasure builds too fast. Too much. I shatter, legs trembling, vision going black at the edges. I scream his name so loud that it echoes off the walls. But he doesn't stop — he only fucks me harder, desperate, wild. My whole body is shaking, every nerve ending alive and raw and tuned to him. He grunts my name — voice heavy with need.

He bites hard into the mark at my neck again, and I feel his orgasm building up through our bond. A hot wave that leaves me dizzy and boneless.

I can feel everything. He's falling apart too, muscles locked, breath coming in ragged bursts. The need to see him undone is riding me like a compulsion. I arch my back as he slams into me, over and over, until I feel him lose it — feel his cock throb and pulse, spilling inside me with a growl that shivers the glass in the windows.

He collapses against me, breath ragged, arms wrapped tight. For a minute, we just stand there together — me pinned to the door, him draped over my back like a hungry beast after a kill. I love this. I love him.

"I should lock you out of the library more often," he pants, still inside me.

"That's a death wish," I purr, pushing my ass back to feel him twitch.

He bites my neck, gentle this time. "I love you, Kassira." I melt. "You're everything," he says, quiet and rough.

I turn in his arms. His shirt is half torn, my skirt rucked up, underwear shredded on the floor. We look like we've been at war.

"I love you too," I whisper and then narrow my eyes. "But next time, if you keep me out of my own library," I say, poking a finger into his chest, "I'm going to let Neris bite you somewhere sensitive."

His eyes gleam silver, and he grins, all fangs and promise. "I'd like to see her try."

I roll my eyes, but can't help smiling. "You're impossible."

"Look who's talking," he says, and kisses me — slow and deep, like we have all the time in the world.

"We should probably clean up," I say, voice soft and happy.

"We could," he says, "or—" He leans in, lips brushing mine, and grabs my ass, fingers digging deep, "—we could stay here and see how many times I can make you come before your surprise is ready."

Seven. Seven times was the answer. In the span of less than an hour. I am completely dickmatized and I don't care. I walk beside Draven down the hallway, grinning foolishly.

The guards posted at the library doors snap to attention and open them wide. Draven bows with mock flourish and gestures me in first.

I smile, but the moment I cross the threshold, the air changes. The smell of old parchment and pine polish hits me, but it's softer. Cozy, almost. The library is... completely different.

I blink, confused. The heavy old tables and rigid straight-backed chairs are gone. In their place — clusters of armchairs in deep jewel tones. Plush things you can sink into and never leave. There are reading nooks built into the window alcoves, each one piled with blankets and pillows. The fireplace is lit, and above it hangs a new portrait. A wolf and a hellhound, tangled together in a playful chase. They look exactly like Neris and Draxis!

A sprawling couch so big it could fit six shifters at once sits at my right. There are even little side tables, each with a stack of notebooks and a basket of sharpened pencils. A tray sits at the end of the couch, already steaming with fresh, dark coffee and a plate of pastries that suspiciously remind me of my old bakery. And in front of the couch, there's a desk. A big, beautiful desk made of dark wood and perfect for writing.

But what catches in my throat isn't the furniture. Or even the coffee and the pastries. It's the shelves. There aren't just books anymore. There are crystal vials, jars of dried herbs, carved runes, delicate little boxes that pulse with old magic. Every inch is filled with something I told Draven about in casual conversation — without any expectations. And more.

I turn to Draven and that's when I see it. Above the door, in curling, hand-carved script, a plaque. KASSIRA'S DEN. Not a library, not a research center. My den.

I stare. I don't move. I don't even know how to breathe anymore.

Draven's hand slides into mine, his thumb tracing over my knuckles.

"You like it?" he asks, and even though he tries to keep the question light, there's an edge to his voice.

I look at him, and there's no smugness. No arrogance. Just hope. Just a man who wants to make his mate happy.

It hits me then — the weight of it all. How much thought, how much care went into making me this space. How even after the world burned and re-formed around us, he still remembered the little things I said in passing. The way I complained about the chairs, the dusty air, the lack of decent light.

I blink rapidly, trying not to cry.

"We can add more books," he says, "or take some away. If you want a bigger window, I'll rip out a wall. Whatever you need."

Neris yips in my head, tail wagging so hard I'm surprised I don't get whiplash. *"He loves us,"* she sings, as if it wasn't obvious.

I just stare for a full, awkward minute. The words are stuck in my throat. I'm still trying not to cry.

He shifts from foot to foot, anxiety climbing. "Is it—if you want the old stuff back, I can—"

I kiss him before he finishes. He stiffens for a second, then melts in, arms winding around me. When I pull back, he searches my face, waiting for me to speak.

"This is perfect," I whisper, brushing his cheek. "You're perfect."

THE END

BONUS

Author's Warning: Blame one of my Wattpad readers for this bonus scene. It takes place while Draven and Kassira were "occupied" in the air after the final battle.

Martin had never been anything more than absolutely normal. A completely common bear shifter. His bear wasn't particularly big or small. Not too grumpy, not too aggressive. Just... a bear.

And Martin? He was just a baker. Owned a modest bakery in town. Not exactly a thrilling success, but it did well enough. His pastries weren't legendary, but they hit the spot when you needed something sweet or savory. His bread wasn't too soft or too crusty. Just good, dependable bread. Like good, dependable Martin.

He'd been surprised — genuinely shocked — when, many months ago, he was invited to provide pastries for one of the royal balls. But he'd said yes, of course. Who wouldn't? Even now, after all this time, Martin still thought about what had happened that night. How his completely ordinary wolf-shifter employee had claimed to be the Alpha King's mate. How the moment had been so mortifying, Martin had nearly prayed to the Moon

Goddess to open the floor and swallow him whole.

He'd assumed he'd never be invited to another royal event again. And he was right. No one ever asked him again — not since poor Kassira was exiled to Kunou Forest. And not since she came back.

Martin didn't know what the hell had happened during that exile. But when Kassira returned, the King suddenly declared her his fated mate. His true mate. Then why had he rejected her in the first place? And why wasn't he mating her today? Why was he bonding with his former girlfriend instead?

Martin was confused. But of course, a low-ranked, ordinary shifter like him had no right to question the King. He wasn't privy to the Royal Family's business. He hadn't even been invited to the mating ceremony. Only the most powerful shifters were. So he just did what he always did — he trusted that the King knew best.

Still, those thoughts swirled in his head as he took the short path home through the forest, after another long day at the bakery. He'd stopped to let his bear out for a few minutes, let him stretch and breathe, and now he was slowly making his way back.

His eyes were fixed on the ground, his mind barely registering the distant screams he'd heard earlier — or the faint scent of smoke and fire still clinging to the trees in the distance.

"The Royal Guards will take care of it," Martin muttered aloud. His bear rumbled in quiet agreement.

His thoughts drifted to the leftover pie waiting for him at home. A nice way to end the day. A sweet little snack before bed. Maybe he'd even add a dollop of cream on top — his bear had a sweet tooth, after all.

Martin's mouth was already watering when — SPLAT! Something wet landed right on the top of his head.

"Oh no," he groaned. "Not another bird poop." That would make it the third time this year.

Birds usually avoided the shifter kingdom of Yelora — too many predators. But for some reason, they couldn't seem to avoid Martin.

With his heart in his throat, he reached up and touched the wet spot on his scalp. Something wasn't right. The consistency… it wasn't like before.

Frowning, Martin looked up, squinting through the trees to spot the offending bird. But it looked like the weirdest bird he'd ever seen.

He called on his bear and sharpened his vision. And froze. Horror clenched tight in his chest.

He looked back down at his hand — now coated in thick, white, gooey liquid. And he dropped to his knees with a strangled noise, frantically rubbing the mess off on every patch of moss he could find.

His bear let out a growl of disbelief. And for the first time in Martin's life, his usually mild-mannered bear took over.

He forced a shift.

Bear Martin didn't hesitate — he just ran. Faster than he'd ever run. All the way home. Not stopping once.

After a very long, nearly scalding shower, Martin and

his bear came to a silent, unanimous conclusion — they would never take the short path home ever again.

And it would be years before they could enjoy pie with cream on top again.

My Other Published Works

If you're a dark romance reader, you might want to give Traitor a try. It's the first book in my Iron Vultures MC series — just be sure to read the trigger warnings first!

"He made me his. Then, he branded me a traitor."

Elyna thought she finally escaped her past. Running from a dangerous MC, she found refuge with the Iron Vultures and in the arms of their ruthless president, Bones. For eight months, she lived a lie - wrapped in his leather, sleeping in his bed, believing she was safe. Believing he loved her.

But secrets have a way of surfacing.

When her past is exposed, Bones doesn't ask questions. He doesn't listen. He marks her. He brands her. And he sends her back to the very men she ran from.

Left for dead, broken beyond repair, Ely swears one thing: if she survives, she will burn it all down.

Now, she has a new name, a new life, and a new purpose. She is no longer the girl who loved a man who betrayed her. She is the woman who will never make the same mistake again.

But Bones?

He isn't done with her.

And he'll do anything to get her back.

You Can Also Find Me On:

TikTok

Facebook

Instagram

Facebook Reader Group

Printed in Great Britain
by Amazon

e97af17d-2a47-48ea-aec9-629000ba58a5R01